A Deed After Death

by

John Mijac

Thanks Tom!

John

Enjoy!

Copyrights

Special thanks to Nancy Wall, Kieran Sikdar, Adam Walters, Laura O'Bagy, Greta Ward Randy Rogers, Laura Mance, and, so many others.

Dedication

This work is dedicated to my long-time companion, the love of my life and my husband, Mitchell L. Black.

Thank you, Mitch, for your unconditional love and for your unwavering belief in me.
Without you, I wouldn't even be here.

Chapter 1: Stranger in a Strange Land

Pari Workingboxwalla collapsed on the three hundred and seventy-nineth step of the Samrat Yantra in the Jantar Mantar; the huge 300 year old sundial in New Delhi. A stranger in a very strange land, he was lost, terrified, and scared of what he had done. He thought he might never find his way back to sanity.

This was the first place his father had brought him when they'd arrived in India. Pari had marveled at the climb to the sun on the outsized dial. "This instrument is accurate to a second!" his dad had said. *Trying to impress me with our glorious ancestors—his old theme*, he'd thought. Today his stomach knotted as he watched the quick movement of the shadow on the dial. *Time is running out.*

When his folks told him he was going to India he'd been excited and relieved. He needed a break from his life. He'd imagined exotic scenes straight out of *Bollywood*, but he hadn't expected to feel the complete foreigner here. He thought he'd take India in stride but the rickshaw ride from the airport to the hotel finished that idea—naked children squatting by the side of the road, pigs running up to devour their shit, old women sweeping dirt streets past piles of cow dung fueling endless roadside cooking fires. Everything seemed foreign, only this enigmatic observatory felt familiar. After his blowup, he'd got himself lost in Delhi till he found himself here.

Damn, I can't believe they thought they could just marry me off. He'd been unaware of their true motive till his mom had brought out pictures of the girl...an arranged marriage had not been part of his vacation plans—but he hadn't planned to tell them he was quitting school either, a shock for a shock. The argument played over as he closed his eyes.

☼

"Get married? What the fuck are you talking about?" Fuck? He'd never cursed in front of them before. He covered, "Mom? Really? Marriage? I can't believe you think I'm going to marry someone I've never met. I'm American." He knew that jibe hurt.

He watched his parents decide who was going to take this on. Father turned away first and took a sip of his Johnny Walker, his mom sighed and smoothed the stiff folds of her new Sari. It was obvious to him she hadn't worn one in quite a while.

"Pari-Jan. You know, language like that is too much upsetting for me. It is very unprofessional."

Pari was ashamed her accent still embarrassed him, but he attacked anyway. "Don't make this about me, it's your attempt to make up for the last twenty years in the U.S. You can't fix it by marrying me off."

"Shame on you, Pari-Jan."
Her lilting, disapproving tone sent him over the edge. He shouted, "Shut up!"

"Bakrichod!" His father's worst curse, it cut. "You don't want what we have given you? You want to make your own way? Good! Then go. Ja! You go, boy. Get out from here. I am done with you."

"Fuck you, you old goat!" He'd slammed the door on the way out covering his shame with anger.

He'd passed through the alabaster lobby toward the hotel gate leading to the *real India*, as he thought. A turbaned Sikh staff member hurried along beside him trying to anticipate his whim — *creepy*. He'd given up trying to talk to the staff; everyone was embarrassed by his attempts to circumvent the caste system, so he'd quickly learned to ignore them, as all the other guests did. It still made him sick. He stopped on his way out the gate and turned to the porter, noticing what a handsome young man he was...bright eyes, intelligent. Pari decided to try again.

"Hey, sorry to make you run after me like this."

"No mention." The fellow looked confused.

"Look, I just need to sit down and cool off. Is there somewhere I can go?" The fellow just shook and nodded his head from side to side in a gesture that looked to Pari as if he were saying both yes and no. That pissed him off again, and he turned and stomped through the gate.

Then he was out on JanPath moving through the crowded stalls set up on the side of the road and threading through the crowds of New Delhi. It was Holi and the streets were packed with revelers throwing colored powders at each other. *What's got into me, who am I, when did this begin?*

However, he knew exactly when the change had started. He hadn't been able to talk to his folks about that any more than he'd been able to keep it from replaying in his mind — that first full moon night he'd done triage in the ER back in Tucson. Until then, medicine had been an intellectual exercise and he'd been good at it—proud of his ability to remember treatments, size up a patient and prioritize needs. He'd been fine with his career choice, until then. Yet after that night he was uncertain of everything except his guilt and shame.

☼

　　　　People had arrived faster that night than the nurses could log them. The ER was short on staff, beds and time, but not on patients. He'd grabbed the charts and walked the rooms, sizing up the needs of the sick and trying to separate out the healthy but needy folk from the truly infirm. The nine year old vomiting in bed one and the belly stab-wound in bed three topped his list. He'd noted two more flu cases in beds seven and four, but they were adults in good shape and he thought they could wait. He saw a drug seeker feigning a headache in bed six, *I am definitely moving him to the end.* The patient that should have been in bed five was up and wandering— dementia. *She's the new number three.*
Then he saw the patient in the hall with the broken leg...a compound fracture, *oops, make that the new three.* He'd noted a dehydrated senior, probably another flu case, in bed four. He'd thought he might need to put her at number four or five. He looked into the lobby and saw it filling up and started to worry. He wasn't ready, not ready to be this busy … nor for the girl who'd been brought in and dumped, wild-eyed-scared and stoned. *Shit, she's higher than a fucking kite.* He knew he had to talk to her but still wished he could put it off.

　　　　"Hey sweetheart, tell me your name." She looked paranoid and frightened.

　　　　"What?"

　　　　"I said, tell me your name."

　　　　"Tell me your name," she echoed.

　　　　I don't have time for this. "Pari is my name," he said, "now what's yours?"

　　　　"I'm quite contrary."

God these people are annoying, "Okay, Contrary what?"

"Pari what?"

"Workingboxwalla, Pari Workingboxwalla" he sighed, "what did you take, Miss Contrary?" His bedside manner took a dive.

"Workingboxwalla, strange name, what's it mean?"

I really don't have time for this. "It means, the man who works the typewriter. What did you take?"

A nurse poked her head into the hall and frowned at him. He knew she thought drug users were vermin, worth little or no attention from her or anyone in the ER, and at the moment he was inclined to agree with her. Miss Contrary started giggling and talking to herself. That did it for Pari, he pushed her bed to the side of the isle and slipped her chart to the bottom of the group. He'd figured she'd just sleep it off like most of the users who came in, but he was wrong. She never woke again. Miss Contrary died in the hour, and that was the last he heard about her...for a while.

No one blamed him but he knew... *All my fault. I killed her.*

☼

A couple of kids were running up the steps, invading his space. It didn't matter, he had to move, he had to get down off this perch, he was hungry and exhausted from rehashing his failures and he needed to....what?

"Arre! Sirkha!" One of the boys said, pushing past him.

"Sorry, I don't speak Hindi." He said, embarrassed at his ignorance.

The smaller one stopped in front of him and laughed. "Not just Hindi, sahib, Marathi. We're on vacation, are you? Where are you from? What is your name?"

The little boy's series of questions in near perfect English made him feel even more inadequate and stupid. It brought his anger right back to the top and he pushed past the boy, hurrying down the steps. He needed something familiar, anything, but he had no clue where to go for that.

He walked back toward where he thought the hotel was but soon got lost in the twisted streets and crowds. A young man shouted "Jai Hind!" while throwing something at him, covering Pari in scarlet powder. A band passed by with horns and drums so loud they almost drowned out the crowd. Young men danced wildly. Bollywood zombies on crack...everything seemed quite insane. Lost in the throng he finally spotted a McDonald's. *Yes*, He thought. *A refuge*.

Still, even this seemed alien. He wanted a hamburger and fries, but that wasn't on the menu. He turned to leave and bumped into an imposing figure. Pari turned his head to curse him, but the smile on the man's face disarmed him instantly. He was everything Pari was not: Anglo, tall, honey blond hair with copper highlights and just a little curl, well-muscled, obviously wealthy—a man of the world. The fellow laughed and spoke as if they were old friends, starting in the middle of a conversation.

"I agree. I could really use something familiar to eat right now."

"You agree?" Pari was too startled to be rude.

"The menu seems more foreign because everything about this place is otherwise so familiar."

"Uh, yes, it's true." Just how did he know I was thinking that?

"Glad we came here though. I don't normally frequent Hamburger joints, but somehow it sounds just right. My name's Cory. Cory Deels."   He stuck out his hand.

Pari shook it automatically. "Pari Workingboxwalla."

"Good to meet you, Pari. How about a McSpicy Paneer and fries?"

"What? Paneer?"

"Don't worry, it's just cheese, fried cheese. I'll bet you've had that." Pari laughed and wondered how this man knew he was not local. "I'm buying."

"Thanks, That would be great...I seem to have left my wallet. But how did you know?"

"Know what?"

"That I'm American."

Cory smiled. "That was the easy part: personal space. You keep two feet open all about you. The average Indian young man only needs an inch or two." Cory smiled, a big and open smile while inviting him to sit in a booth and chat. It seemed like fate, especially once they realized they were both from Tucson.

"What a grand coincidence!" Cory exclaimed. He told Pari he'd come to India looking for his son, who'd disappeared in an ashram. Pari told Cory about the argument with his folks.

"Parents need forgiveness too. We all make mistakes."

"Yeah, but I haven't told them everything, there are a few things I just can't talk to them about."

"Believe me, I understand."

"They won't understand when I don't go back to Med school. The idea of it makes me sick." He told him the story about the young girl who'd died on his watch, but Cory seemed unmoved.

"What did you expect? People die every day and you can't be responsible for their actions."

"That's true, but I've lost my stomach for it, and I have no clue what I'm going to do for money, or a place to live, any of it."

"Money should be the least concern of yours right now; you are making decisions about the course of your life, but no place to live?"

"My dad owns the duplex where I room; he made it clear I can only stay there while I go to school."

"That strikes me to the quick. Everyone should have a place of their own. I am a REALTOR after all."

Now Pari laughed, "So you want to sell me a house? I can't afford one." Pari took a sip of his soda, rolling the straw wrapping paper into a tiny ball. *Still, I can't go crawling back to dad.*

"Not my suggestion, I have an idea. My son made it clear he was not coming home, so, for the time being I have an extra room. Also, my business has increased to the point where I need an assistant. I propose when you return to Tucson you stay at my place until you find your feet. You must do my bidding in exchange for the room and board I provide…nothing beyond what a Workingboxwalla would do for a Brit in the old days."

Pari wondered how he knew what his name meant, forgetting he had told him in the story of Miss Contrary. "So, you want a secretary?"

"No, a man Friday, I need an assistant."

"Don't think you'll convert me, I have no interest in sales."

"Sales are the least of what a REALTOR does. Speaking of that, you will need to take real estate classes because I'll need you to be licensed; I'll pay for them and pay you a wage if you promise me six month's service. That will get you through the end of this year and solidly into the next. If it's not for you, then go your way, but you might find you like Real Estate. If you do, we'll renegotiate. When are you headed back?"

"Tomorrow, if I have a choice."

"Give me your number, I'll text you where to go and who to talk to...I'll be back in town in a few weeks."

The man was magnetic and, though it seemed odd to Pari that Cory would give him such an opportunity, he accepted.

Chapter 2: A Broker's Responsibility

Cory Deels tapped the rickshaw driver on the shoulder and motioned for him to pull over to the tea stall on the side of the road. The drone from three wheeled vehicle cycled down, as they bumped off the Tarmac and into the rutted ground that served as the parking lot.

He'd spent the last three weeks in a vain effort to get his son to return with him. After meeting Pari, he thought he owed his son another chance, but no dice. When he got to the Ashram he'd been told Raphie, his son, was keeping silence, so Cory waited, staying at a local hotel, seeing the local sights, until the spiritual discipline was over. When he returned his son still refused to see him. What a waste.

His phone dinged, letting him know another contract document had arrived to review. *Pain in the bloody ass!* Cory was required, by law, to review every contractual document any of his agents created, within 10 days! It didn't matter where he was, it still had to be done.

He had appointed one of his agents to take over for him in his absence, but the fellow had quit a week ago. He sighed, reviewing it on his phone...happily all was well and he could approve it and move on. *I need help!*

He extracted himself from the tiny vehicle and carefully threaded his way through parked motorcycles, bullock carts, other rickshaws, bicycles and a crowd of young men watching a cricket match on a cellphone--a shout went up after a score. *Glad their game is going well. This trip has been a bust!* Cory was having a hard time not descending into a deeply sour mood. He sat down on a rugged stool next to at a blue painted wooden table in the dust. The Chai-Walla stopped by, rubbing the surface with a filthy rag while dropping a cup and saucer on the table with the other hand.

"Chai, sahib?"

"Umm...do you have coffee?"

"No sahib, sanka yes, coffee no. Chai best, sahib."

"Okay, chai then."

"Teek, okay." The fellow produced a huge aluminum tea pot and, from three feet above the cup, poured a stream of steaming golden liquid into it without spilling a drop.

Normally, Cory would have worried about the hygiene in such a place, but he was bone tired, depressed, and decided a spot of tea wouldn't kill him. *Besides, I'm on my way back home. Even if I do get sick I can deal with it in the states.* He sipped his tea and marveled at how much better the syrupy brew made him feel. His driver was standing with the kids, leaning over one of the boys, almost right on top of him, watching the game while deftly sipping tea from a saucer. A louder cheer went up from the crowd.

Two young boys ran through the dust and up to Cory, they had been watching his every move from the edge of the gathering and must have decided he was no threat. He grinned at them and made a face, they both laughed and the older one stepped closer.

"Tumce nauw kai?" Cory shrugged, making an "I don't understand you" face.

The younger one pushed his friend aside shouting "Gupna!" The child stood up straight and asked, "What is your name?"

Cory, grinned back at them. "Cory. What is your name?"

"Madza Nau...My Name is Rajanath! Baksheesh sahib?"

Cory knew what that meant and began to dig in his pocket for some change, but the shop owner had spotted the kids and came flying at them with a stick.

"Ja! Go! Get out of here!" He shouted and the two ran while laughing. Cory could see this was obviously a routine that had played out many times before.

"Sorry, sahib, these beggar children, don't give them a paisa, not one cent. More chai?"

Cory nodded as his phone rang...*the office.*

"Cory Deels, Evy, is that you?"

"Yeah Boss, things are falling apart here. When are you coming back?"

"My flight leaves tomorrow. How could things be so bad? We just talked yesterday."

"How about a complaint raised with the Real Estate Commissioner about Sam." Sam was the agent that had quit. "One of his clients says Sam neglected his fiduciary duty to him. She sent a letter to the Commissioner."

"That's bloody unlikely, Sam's a good agent. Send me the letter and I'll review it, get an extension and decide on a course of action." Cory had never really liked Sam as a person, but professionally he knew Sam's work was always above board.

"Also, there's a fellow calling who says he's one of ours. Just graduated and apparently you recruited him."

"Okay, so sign him up and email me his employment agreement...standard split."

"There's a problem, the Commissioner says he needs a provisional license, apparently he has a past. He says you okayed his hire."

"What? Who is this agent?"

"Pari Workingboxwalla. Do you know him?"

"I do, damn-it." *How could that be?* Cory valued his intuition and was rarely wrong about people. "Tell him to hold on, Evy, I have faith in that lad, I'd trust him even if he was accused of murder."

"Okay, Cory, you're in charge. You're the Broker."

Chapter 3: A Return to Insanity

After meeting Cory, Pari had gone back to the Imperial Palace to apologize to his folks—though it seemed to do no good—so he picked up his bags, his passport and returned to the states that day. His dad had given him three weeks to clear out of the duplex, though he could have done it in a day. Now, those three weeks were over and it was time to move, though he didn't feel ready. He knew that was mostly mood, not a lack of boxes. Looking around the bleak flat now, he realized there was little to move. *What of me is there to pack?* Pari realized that for years he'd thought about little besides his studies and getting through med-school. He hadn't even allowed himself hobbies unless they were academic. Then, after med-school was off the list and he'd returned to the states he'd jumped right into a crash course in Real Estate. Ninety hours of memorizing terms was a snap for Pari. He'd doubled up on day and night classes and had done it all, plus taking the test, in a week and a half, the school said it was a record. Pari called the brokerage when he passed, but the woman there had said he'd need to wait for Cory's return to begin. That would be tomorrow and Pari hoped he'd be impressed.

He pushed a stack of books off the spindly metal chair in the dining area to the floor and sat down at the littered table, sorting through the pile of mail and old homework. Realizing there was nothing in the pile of any value he dumped the lot into the trash can. *What have I done?* He knew he'd changed his future irrevocably, and possibly not for the better. He couldn't breathe. Then someone knocked at the door. Opening it, he saw Dorothea Samaniego, the last person he expected or wanted to see. She stuck her foot in the door and guffawed.

"Workingboxwalla, you look like shit." She laughed again, "Still, you're pretty cool, even if you did dump me on the first date."

Seeing her again was a return to insanity … all the things he could not face came back with a vengeance. Her ironic smile brought him back to the day he'd met her, at one of his "journal" sessions, when he was still in school.

☼

Every week the interns at University Medical Center would get together to decompress, read their notes and their journals to each other and share a beer. Pari noticed Dorothea the moment she walked in. She was cute, smart and just about his size, wore her hair short and wild, in a boyish cut that complimented her jeans, boots and cowgirl outfits. The haircut made her eyes seem larger, like those weeping children in velvet paintings. Her nature, though, had nothing to do with sad. Pari had found her exciting and confusing, unlike any other girl he'd known. She'd come to the journal session with one of the other interns, but made it clear that she was on no one's arm. Her wit was sharp and irreverent. He realized now she'd played him from the start and that she knew even then how confused he was.

"Workingboxwalla," she said, "never change it, great name!" He flushed. No one had ever complimented him on his name.

"I'm Dorothea Samaneigo, and that's a mouthful too. Just call me Dory." He was too embarrassed to answer, but she let it go and cut into the general conversation about blood pressure and drugs as if she were one of the interns.

While she was making the rounds Rupert, one of Pari's friends, said she was majoring in anthropology, but liked crossing boundaries. Then he said, "Too bad about her sister."

"Sister?" Pari asked.

"Different as night and day, Mary and Dory, but they were close, real close. Mary died a bit ago." Pari shrugged the remote death off, glancing at Dory again, she was laughing.

It seemed to Pari as though she knew he'd asked about her and approved. Still, it was strange to hear her laugh at the moment her sister's death had been mentioned. That sent a chill down his spine. Later, the crowd moved on to club DV8, switching juice and coffee for vodka and beer. The music was good, the booze flowed and everyone let loose—as if they were all ready for something new. Dory might have picked any one of them, but she chose him—a virgin, an innocent. He was certain she knew. He was soused and was sure that too was obvious. Dory caught him looking at her, and again she laughed.

"How about you and me splitting?"

"What?" He pretended he couldn't hear her over Rivers Cuomo singing "I was Scared."

"C'mon Pari, we're gone." She'd grabbed his hand and pulled him from the building. Before he knew it they were on the road, heading out into the desert. It was exhilarating. She'd had an old military jeep, no windows but the front shield, two seats, green of course, and a rough interior. He could see the road through a rusted hole in the passenger floorboard. The thing must have been almost seventy years old, but it ran like a dream. The air whipping around the screen was chilly, the moon full and brilliant. She'd turned off the headlamps when they'd left the main road. She knew to drive fast enough to skim the vehicle over the dirt washboard. Dust plumed far behind.

"Where are we going?" he'd shouted.

"What's it matter?"

He watched in amazement and with a little fear as they flew past the dark forms of saguaros standing by the side of the road. The giant cactus's seemed to be marching off into darkness. *It's like a scene from Tolkien, maybe the meeting of the Ents.* They hit a bump and left the earth for a moment, skidding and fish tailing when they returned to the earth. He shouted, exhilarated, she laughed, and then pulled over and slowed. They came to a rough turnoff and headed right up a dry wash flanked by dirt cliffs on either side. She got out and turned the hubs, putting the jeep into four wheel.

They moved very slowly after that, but it was no less exciting. Up over boulders that seemed larger than the jeep, sometimes creeping along the side of the arroyo so tilted he'd thought they would topple. At last they came to an exit from the wash and mounted the flank of a hill.

"Wait here." She said as she shut the jeep off and jumped out.

In a few minutes she pulled together a pile of dead mesquite and lit a fire. *The girl is a wonder.* By the light of it he'd guessed this was a place many had come before. He saw blackened rocks and melted glass in an old fire pit. Casings and old shells were strewn around the site.

Then Dory looked at him and grinned. "Time for fun!"

He watched in amazement as she pulled out a small bottle full of white powder and a razor blade and spread a couple of lines on the jeep's fender. He broke out in a sweat. He had never tried cocaine—any drugs—before. He wasn't judgmental; he was terrified he might really like them. Dory, though, was obviously a pro; she pulled half a plastic straw out of her pocket and in a flash, two of the four lines were gone. She turned and handed him the straw. He looked at it stupidly.

"Ummm, I've never..."

"Give me a break. Just suck it up your nose, it's not going to kill you."

He wasn't too sure about that, but did as he was told. The cocaine burned like acid but only for a moment, and then his head exploded. White heat filled his brain and then coursed through his body. He had no idea that the air could feel so sensual, that the touch of his shirt could be a caress. Everything made sense to him then: their being together, the parched desert plants, the dust in the air, even his skin color and hers—they matched, like cream poured into coffee but not stirred. The promise of a mixture, a stirring, tantalized him. He saw in an instant, that everything in life had a reason, or so it seemed. He had to tell this to Dory, who now seemed to be his most intimate companion. Words spilled out as he cleverly explained everything. He felt he had the gift of tongues and used it. She laughed ... she knew the thrill of the first time user, and joined in the talk. It seemed more meaningful and intimate than anything he had ever known.

Too soon the feelings began to fade and she cut a few more lines. They began their discussions again, but he noticed there were forbidden areas. Any mention of family and Dory changed the topic —except for once, when he asked her directly about her folks.

She said, "That's the way it is. You do one wrong thing, it's over. They figure out who they think you are and then kick you out." That rang a bell.

She changed in a flash from fun and wild to wildly furious. She seemed angry with him for asking and he didn't want her anger, above all things. He wasn't sure how to fix it. He murmured something in sympathy but she rolled on, unstoppable.

"Then the whole truth comes out. She lied to me, Pari. I should have known. I'm adopted. Mary, my sister, well I guess she's not my sister, we don't, we never looked like twins, so I guess I should have known. She had my mother's, my..." Dory floundered then, clearly at a loss to find the right words. "She had Dolores'...Shit, she had my ex-mother's eyes, I didn't. I don't know how I could have been so blind. My mom, my dad....God, I don't even know what to call them. They met in Japan, when he was on duty. He was in the Air Force."

Pari was confused. "Japan?"

"I know, too much information, but the point is, she's half Japanese, half Anglo, grew up in an orphanage. Isn't that ironic, she's an orphan and I am too. I guess at least we have that in common. I figured I just took after Dad more than her, but I can see that's not true either. I tried talking to them, but it only made things worse. Much worse. We've always fought, but not like this. Then, then I got to meet her … Ms. Michaels, my biological mother … like it's supposed to be some present. I meet my real mom, the one who abandoned me, threw me out like garbage, and that's supposed to be fun for me? How did she think it would make me feel? Big argument, big. Dad had a heart attack, and he died. First Mary, then Dad."

She stopped, looking out to the desert and then began again, "All my fault. Shit, my whole life turned to crap and I don't get anything but grief from anybody—grief and death. I'm glad I'm out of there." Pari had started to say something but she'd put her hand right over his mouth. She did it with such force he'd winced, thinking she was going to slap him. "Don't. Just don't. I don't want to say one more word about this." Her mood had turned in a moment and she pulled two beers out of the cooler and laughed, "Here's to independence!"

They talked and laughed till the first hint of dawn. As that first light showed him their surroundings, he found her touching his body. Her touch was unlike any he had known before, hot and full of electricity. He had a raging hard-on. From the drugs, from her touch, at that moment he didn't care. Her lips went down on him and it was hot and wet and sweet. He'd never experienced anything like it. He pulled her up then, and their lips met. He couldn't tell where hers began and his ended, but the scent and taste of his cock on her lips had made him even more excited. It had also embarrassed and shamed him, but somehow he pushed those feelings away.

His whole body was as sensitive as his penis and their lovemaking seemed to go on forever...but it didn't. As he watched the first rays of the sun strike the Sawtooth Mountains across the valley, all that juice and joy dried up in a moment. He was naked, exhausted, shriveled and cold on a barren rock and consumed in guilt and paranoia. *This is what crashing feels like*, he thought. Dory was standing by the jeep, licking her finger to wipe the fender of every trace of powder. They had long ago emptied the bottle; there was nothing left. She began to talk to herself and Pari couldn't help but listen.

"I'm sorry, Mary, so sorry… Mary, quite contrary. I shouldn't have left you at that damn hospital" The words had hit him like a bullet. She sat down and began to weep, looking away from him, shaking. He knew now he should have gone to her, but he'd realized then with a shock that Miss Contrary, the girl he had killed with his negligence, was Dory's sister. Shaky and confused, wrapped in his own guilt, Pari sat down and began to weep.

It was then he'd seen the tracks on her thighs, between her toes—purple blotches recording past use by someone together enough to hide it. He'd seen this before in the ER. Track marks on heroin users who had overdosed when they'd found a bigger vein than they were used to, or a more potent fix. She disgusted him. *Dory killed her, she gave her the drugs, she's the reason her sister died, not me.*

He watched her looking for more drugs and wanted to throw up. He had to be rid of her soon. She was pitiful, alone and as guilty, a shadow of herself and in need, but that didn't matter to him then. He saw her only as an addict, a user who had pulled him into a place he should never have gone and so he'd fixed all his guilt and blame on her. He threw her clothes at her then and told her, "Get dressed, I have a class. We've got to get going." Pari drove the jeep back to town and let himself out at his duplex without one more word to her.

Now she was here again, and she'd brought a friend.

Chapter 4: A Shift in Perspective

Pari stood, gut rolling, remembering the entirety of their first meeting in the moments between opening the door and her comment, "...Even if you did dump me on the first date..." stung. *I'm no less guilty.* "Really? Was it a date?" He said, trying to banter with her—he knew it wasn't working. "Who's your friend?"

"Pari, Spike; Spike, this is Pari, but you can call him Doctor Workingboxwalla."

He saw her look change...she knew. It seemed to him again that Dory knew more than she had a right to know. *She's an enigma, I should probably shut the door now.*

"Okay" she continued, "I can see that career went out the window—as it should have."

"What?" *What does she mean? Damn her.*

"Workingbox, you told me last time we were together you hated medicine." He didn't remember saying that. She smiled, he remembered that smile, dangerous.

"Looks like a case of selective amnesia. Well, I have the cure."

With that she pushed her way in and Spike followed. Pari closed and locked the door, knowing what was coming. Spike stood while Dory cut a few lines. Spike looked at Pari like a man thinking about buying a new car, Pari was the floor model.

He knew he should have said no and told them to go, but the ache in his heart knocked the wind out of him. That sour memory of her should have ended things, but he pushed it aside and it faded quicker than a bad dream. With it went caution and any thought of shame at Mary quite contrary's death. This time Dory didn't mind talking about her adoptive mother, but what she said about Dolores Samaniego was harsher than anything Pari would have ever said about his folks. Yet she seemed so full of guilt over Mary's death it sounded as though she thought her mom was right to blame her. *Why is it we can so easily see the faults of others?*

Then there was Spike. To Pari, he was Dory in every way but one. Handsome, tough-looking but handsome in the eyes, beautiful skin with just a touch of stubble on the chin...black leather, muscled, smart. He smelled of bay leaves, cloves, and musk—Pari found him intoxicating. Spike was open and engaging and after a line, Pari fell under his spell. At least that's how he wanted to remember it. At first Pari was shy, even coy...but after a little coke—Bam! They were all instant friends, solving life's problems. He poured out everything, India, the disaster with his folks, quitting school, everything except one *contrary* fact.

Pari didn't know how they all ended up in bed together. He couldn't have gone there without the drugs, but go he did. He let Dory play the bridge, always keeping her body between his skin and Spike's. When they both kissed her, their lips and tongues found common ground. Spike's mouth was hot, salty-sweet and irresistible to him. Dory pushed them together, expressing her delight. At first all was excitement and passion, but things changed, the balance moved. The boys began to grapple with each other, their hot smooth skin sliding, sweat to tongue, cheek to cock...together with no separation now.

Their heat rose and Pari was about to cum when he became aware of Dory sitting on the edge of the bed, watching. He cooled in an instant. They took a break for another line and conversation, but guilt crept into Pari's mind. *A tripod may be the most stable structure in nature, but in bed it tips...someone gets left out.* He could see that Dory knew she'd become the third unstable leg, and she wasn't taking it well. Out of nowhere she brought up that final night with her sister, blaming herself and Spike. *Damn, I can't believe she's bringing up her sister again.*

"Why did you let me do it, Spike? Why did you let me give it to her?"

Spike turned away from her as he said, "I couldn't stop you."

Pari was confused, "What are you talking about?"

Dory spoke up, "Mary, my sister. I had a bag and we were getting stopped by the cops. I let her take it and she swallowed it."

"A bag? They were your drugs! Why didn't you come in with her?" Pari shouted, Dory shrunk as if he had hit her.

"What are you talking about?"

"If you'd have come in and told me what was going on, we could have, I could have saved her..." He stopped, knowing he had said way too much.

Dory slapped him and stopped his blurting. She grabbed her things, stopping at the door. She turned and her cold, black eyes burned into Pari.

"Fuck you, Workingbox." She focused on Spike, "You coming?" Spike didn't move, "Fine!" She slammed the door behind her.

Spike held him while he wept. His embrace seemed right, wholesome, though only a short while ago it would have seemed perverse. *A change in perspective makes the mountain into a molehill,* he thought.

Spike stayed the night. Pari's last night in the flat before moving into Cory's house. Neither of them talked about Mary or Dory, or anything else. The human comfort was enough and Pari needed to let his mind turn off.

Later that night he remembered where he had seen Spike before—at the hospital, where he was a part of the cleanup crew. He had suspected then the young man had some other business at the hospital. It turned out he was right. It was a business that led to murder.

Chapter 5: The Broker on Convent

Where am I? Pari thought, rubbing sleep-encrusted eyes. *What happened last night?* He sat up on the rock hard bed, hitting his head on the cement slab above. That nearly put him back down. Nevertheless, he stayed awake and looked around. A concrete floor, florescent light, steel toilet, and bars completed the picture: *in Tucson, in jail, for murder* ... it all came back. He got up and stretched, relieving himself in the can. *Breathe, center, focus.* He yawned. *My version of yoga.* He thought.

"You go, boy!" He mocked himself with a laugh.

It all seemed so unreal to him. *Good God, how did I get here? How can I keep from being tried for a murder I didn't commit? What will people think?* He'd placed a call to the brokerage, when he'd been booked last night, but had to leave a message. Cory almost never took calls off hour—he valued his privacy and jealously guarded it—but Pari was sure he would help when he was able. He thought back to the beginning of this mess, six months ago, to the beginning of his Real Estate Career. The week he'd moved into Cory Deels' house, the day he'd met Woody Madrone. He'd been complaining to Cory, about prospecting for clients. He'd said that he thought people didn't care about him being a Real Estate agent.

☼

"People only care when you care, Pari. Give me no excuses. If you don't love what you do, how do you expect anyone to love you doing it?"

"That's the problem. It's not *what* I'm saying, it's that I don't believe it." Pari sighed and picked up his fork.

They were at Cory's home, on Convent and 18th, down in the barrio on the South side of Tucson. Pari knew the old sections of Tucson well, from Barrio Historico to Armory park. For him, as for many others, Barrio Viejo was the Barrio. The houses there were large and uncommon, but the Deels compound was unique. Years ago, Cory Deels had bought most of the block from Convent to Meyer. The Meyer side was the business, the Convent side, the Deels' residence.

They were sitting in the drawing room going over brokerage rules and duties. Normally this wouldn't happen inside Deel's private quarters, but Cory had decided to celebrate Pari's 6 month licensing. Cory said that it was an important event because most agents had not made a single sale by then and had only just learned the ropes. Apparently, surviving even such a short time was an accomplishment.

Cory served carnitas and salsa fresca on homemade blue corn tortillas, with a Bohemia. A simple meal, but perfectly prepared. Pari had learned that one of Cory's avocations was fine cooking. He was hoping to chill and really celebrate, but that's not the Deels' style. Cory had just finished telling him he needed to keep a journal when the door bell rang.

They both ignored it and continued their conversation.

"Mr. Deels, this isn't surgery or rocket science. I just quit med school and I'm not a fool. I'm looking for a little more freedom, not more homework."

Cory scowled at him, "Don't be an idiot. First, I want you to stop with the Mr. I am not your father nor your teacher, even if I am almost old enough to fit either role. Next, I am suggesting this for your own protection, not for busy work."

"Okay. But I really don't see where a journal will protect me."

"It is a written testament that the memory alone cannot possibly provide. Memorialize everything! You might regret not keeping a journal one day if you are deposed for a trial."

The bell rang again. Deels looked down at the screen. "Confound it!" Cory was annoyed because he went to great lengths to limit work to business hours. Pari was already familiar with the routines. People who visited his house unannounced got a chilly reception. If they rang the bell on Convent, Cory Deels' home, after trying the Brokerage on a Sunday, that was a big no. However, sometimes clients didn't take no for an answer, so he had set up an elaborate security system. Usually Cory was aware of visitors long before they suspected. He even often greeted them before they rang the bell, but not this time.

The first time Pari had come to the house on Convent, he'd found it quite imposing, with its high, block-long buckskin colored facade. That severe wall is broken only by four barred windows and a grand entrance in the center. Ornate, hand carved Corbels hold up an enormous beam supporting the portico. People raise their hands to ring the bell, but the gates silently open before they ring. It is startling. When visitors walk into the pasadizo, the breezeway into the central courtyard, the gate quickly closes behind them. Inside, they are confronted by enormous, closed iron gates in front and behind, filigreed in wild patterns. The chamber is dimly lit by inset sconces. These are flicker like old candles about to extinguish. Small, backlit wrought iron sculptures of twisted human forms frame each sconce. The flickering makes them dance. The gates echo this theme, like some vision of hell. On the South, inset into the ocher plastered wall, a hand-carved mesquite door dwarfs any visitor, it is the entrance to the formal drawing room. Unannounced arrivals find

"Chingada madre! Open this damn door, Cory Deels, or I'll open it and screw your castle."

Cory growled something beneath his breath and spoke to the monitor, "It is Sunday, blast it. Come back tomorrow."

"To hell with that." Pari saw the man reach in his pocket and, zap, the door opened. Cory, who had been standing until then, fell back in his seat.

The roles were reversed. When that humongous door had first opened for Pari, he'd been unprepared for the sight. His eyes had adjusted to the dimly lit pasadizo, so the light from the white plaster behind the door had blinded him. Long past the entrance to the enormous room there was a massive hand-carved stone fireplace, centered in the wall across from the entrance and flanked by two enormous paintings. They'd reminded Pari of murals by Diego Riviera he'd studied in college, but Cory later explained that they'd been done by an anonymous W.P.A. artist in the early 30s. On the left, Tohono O'odham people work in the desert making baskets and pots and harvesting saguaro fruit with their long sticks. The painting on the right celebrated Padre Kino's arrival on a horse, 300 years ago.

Pari had openly gawked when he'd first arrived, totally intimidated, but the man who entered now seemed utterly indifferent.

Cory said, "Woody, this is my assistant, Pari. Pari, this is Woodrow Zapate Madrone."

The man turned to Pari, giving him the look a big dog gives a rabbit. Woody Madrone towered over him at roughly twice his weight. He was probably 40 years older than Pari but the young man had no doubt that giant could crush his skull with one hand. Woody's pockmarked face was as dark as the mud of the Santa Cruz River, sun weathered, leathery, and ruddy on the nose. He stuck out a meaty paw and Pari put his thin, soft hand in the middle of that grip and winced as Woody shook it to the bone.

"Cabrón. Where'd ya pick this little pup up Deels? He's scared shitless."

"India, if you would know, but that is a long tale I will not tell today."

"You and me—habalmos, we've got business, and this inepta cannot listen in."

Cory stared at him. "He's my agent and bound by the same confidentiality I am. I owe you for installing this surveillance system, but that debt was canceled by your forced entry. I'd call the constables but the benefit of our old friendship protects you—for today. He shall stay."

Woody closed his grip a bit tighter, and Pari's knuckles ground against each other. He yipped. Woody smiled an evil grin.

"Claro que si, he has some guts and does not yield, but ... I bind you, Paaari," The slow drawl of his name made Pari shiver. "I bind you now to remain silent over all I say this evening. So pena de muerte, on pain of my certain penalty." Pari looked at Cory in some confusion but Cory just laughed.

"Don't worry, Pari, he won't harm you."

Pari pulled his hand back with some doubt.

"Amigo," Cory said to Woody, "I will not place that burden on this youngster. He shall leave us."

Cory waved Pari out. He took the French doors out to the courtyard, walking slowly toward his quarters, pausing at the fountain. He saw the two men go through the secret passage behind the painting of Father Kino into the media room. That was the last he was supposed to hear of their conversation.

☼

Pari broke from his revere then, still stuck in jail...amazed by the clarity of his memory of that day. He thought his remembrance had been made stronger by yesterday's meeting, when he saw that powerful man undone by death. *A powerful man indeed*, he thought. Mostly he remembered the bullets, the surging blood and a failing heart. That and seeing himself, as if he were in a movie, working his useless emergency room training, and seeing it prove ineffective.

Chapter 6: The Catacombs

Pari stretched and walked around the cramped holding cell. Breakfast had just been brought in, so he knew it must be 6:00 AM. He had no appetite and left the tray on the sink. He couldn't keep that bloody scene out of his head. His life had changed in radical and unpleasant ways even if he could prove his innocence. Officer Moreno, the police officer who had interviewed him yesterday, seemed to think his guilt was a given fact. Once Moreno began piling up the circumstantial evidence, Pari sound guilty, even to himself. *A jury will have no doubt. What can I do?*

He knew his only chance was to review all the events that might be related to the murder. Yet, so much had happened. *Where is the thread I can pull to unravel this web and prove my innocence?* He thought back to the first week at the brokerage, and what he heard the day he met Woody Madrone.

☼

After being dismissed by Cory, Pari walked out to the courtyard. In Southwestern style, Cory's house and its covered porches surround a central courtyard. He stopped in front of the oversized marble fountain in the very center, waiting there, admiring the desert and tropical plantings, until he knew for certain the men had gone to the media room tucked into the Southeast corner of the house. Then he hurried to his rooms on the opposite end of the compound.

Pari ran because he knew it would take some time to get back to where he could hear any conversation. The media room was totally soundproofed except for one area, under the floor. Pari knew a secret. In his quarters, to the side of his bath, is a laundry room with a trap door that leads to tunnels under the house. Cory told him they'd been built by a defrocked Franciscan architect named Brother Adrian in 1915. Brother Adrian had some heretical ideas involving a little free love and lots sex for sale that couldn't see daylight a century ago. The tunnels were hideaways for the ladies, for drink and other illicit activities. Now they were largely abandoned but used for some of the building's infrastructure—and they went everywhere.

He made his way through them and took a passage to the South, lighting it with his phone. The tunnels are cramped and winding, but easy to negotiate and just tall enough for Pari to run if he ran stooped. He took the final bend and heard the rumbles of an argument. Cory's voice dominated, but it barely surpassed the intruder's.

"No! I won't do it."

"Son of a bitch, Deels, after all these years you'd finally get even with the bitch."

"This is not about me, or her, it's all you. I'll have nothing to do with it."

"I've engaged you, cabron. You're my agent now, you have to obey."

"You're wrong. My duty to the law and to disclose supersedes any duty of loyalty to you."

"Estupideces. You are making this crap up."

"Hardly, It's immoral, illegal, unethical, and I won't risk my life and livelihood for such a thing."   .

"Vato, you will do it or maybe I will tell."

Tell what? Pari wondered. Then Cory thundered, "Get out. Go find someone else to list your house. You have lost your honor and my friendship. I am finished with you."

"Maricon de mierda! You will regret this," replied Madrone.

"On a cold day. Get out of my house."

"Cuidado! You are not finished with me you son of a bitch!"

Pari heard Señor Madrone slam the door between the media and dining rooms, stomp down the passage to the living room, and head out through the pasedizo. His heavy footfalls echoed in the tunnels. Then Pari's phone dinged with a text. *Shit, I forgot to turn it off*, he thought, hoping Cory hadn't heard it. He looked down to see the text was Cory's:

"Get back up here. We need to talk."

"k," Pari typed. *Not good*, he thought. *Did he hear me, or was he telling me it was okay to return?* He knew it wouldn't be good to be caught eavesdropping on his employer and landlord. "Busy. Finishing up. brb, boss," he sent back, then trotted back through the passage.

☼

Pari opened his eyes and looked around the holding cell, now hungry for that breakfast. It was cold, but he didn't care, he was famished. While he ate the gruel and cold scrambled eggs, he thought through what he had learned from remembering the events. There was a lot he could deduce now in retrospect:

* Woody had built the security system.

* The two of them were old friends.

* They shared a secret, something Cory didn't want revealed.

* Woody wanted to list his house with Deels Realty, but Cory had refused him. What real estate agent does that? What was his boss hiding?

Despite being in jail, Pari felt excited about this process. It amazed him that he could learn so much by reexamining his own experiences, and he wondered what else he might discover. He turned his mind back to that day again, picking up just as he remembered coming out of the trap door and into his rooms.

☼

He climbed out of the laundry trapdoor and stopped for a moment at the mirror to brush off the dust. He didn't want to give away his skulking in the passages, but it was all for naught. When he walked into his bedroom Cory was already there, he was sitting in the chair by the beehive fireplace, having a conversation on his cell with his I.T. guy, Johnny West. Cory doesn't claim to know everything, but he makes it a habit to know someone who knows whatever he doesn't. Johnny is one of those experts.

From Cory's end of the conversation Pari could tell he was making sure no one would be able to open those doors again without his permission.

"...and I can control it from the net? So if I use this encryption, can someone...can you hack it? ... What if I loose the password? Okay then, I will not loose it. Thank you, Johnny. Yes, of course I owe you a dinner, but you will also see a check in the mail. No, I insist." He hung up and then focused on his iPhone, working on one of the aps. Without looking up, he told Pari to sit down and indicated the other chair. Pari took the bed instead.

"Whatcha want, boss man?"

"One thing would be for you to sit over here with me, so we can have a conversation. An honest conversation one on one. The second would be to quit calling me boss man. You are an independent contractor. I am your broker, not exactly your boss."

"Not exactly the man says. Yes sir, Mr. Deels."

"You are a whelp. As I told you before, if you are going to live in my house, share the fruits of my labor and eat meals with me, you are to call me Cory. I intend to be more your friend than superior."

"Yes, sir. Okay, I mean, yes Cory."

"Also, don't play me for a fool ever again, or friendship will be out of the question."

Pari decided candor might be called for at this point. "I'm sorry, I just thought...."

"You thought you could spy without being caught. Don't dissemble, young man. If you are to be my assistant and my friend you must be candid with me. We must work together and that requires trust. I am not looking for a toady and I am not a fool. I knew you were in the tunnels and that you heard some part of what was said. What you heard is unimportant to me. What is important is whether you are willing to stand up and be honest, are you?" Pari nodded. "Good, but first, admit you were snooping."

Pari took this in for a moment, then realized Cory was offering him something he had never had—an honest and open relationship with another man. Pari certainly had not had that kind of relationship with men, even his own father. He wondered if Cory had a motive. Then, ashamed of his cynicism, he thought, *This could be a man I might admire and perhaps even learn from*. Pari came clean, completely.

"Yes, I was snooping. I was doing my best to find out what you were hiding, or perhaps what he was hiding."

"Thank you. No doubt we all have things to hide, and I will not tell you all of my secrets. However, I propose to be honest with you about what I do reveal. That is a different thing. I may not tell you everything, but what I tell you will always be true. This is a solemn promise from me. You should also know that anything you tell me privately will be kept confidential. I am asking the same of you. If you can do that, I will never snoop and I will treat all you say as truth. Also, I will stand behind your every word. Are you ready for such a commitment?"

Who is this man? His natural defenses dropped. That was scary for him. *Why do I feel ready to follow him to the ends of the earth?* He spoke impulsively. "Yes, I promise you that with all my heart." He thought his voice sounded too earnest. Cory just laughed and stretched out a hand while he stood. *He's so tall, as if he walks above the ground, untroubled by gravity.* They shook.

"That is the way, lad, that is the way. We are off to a good start." Cory looked around the room. "You know, Pari, you are free to pack this stuff up and make this room your own space...your choice. I don't believe Raphael, my son, will ever return here." He paused a moment and then, turning quickly, he spoke as he walked. "Now, tomorrow we will talk about getting your first clients." With that, Cory was out the door. They did speak later and that conversation led Pari to his first clients—the clients who led him into involvement in a murder.

☼

Pari opened his mind again to the harsh reality of jail. What had he learned? Not much more, but his unease had increased. Knowledge is a two edged sword; sometimes it is easier to be ignorant. Thanks to Cory, Pari had taken a new path...*or maybe no thanks, since that path led to this cell*. He couldn't shake the feeling that he was missing something, but what? Pari felt awed by Cory and proud to have gained such a friend, so perhaps he had remembered Cory's part with prejudice. Now, looking back on the incidents that had brought him to this cell, he wondered what it all meant—then and now. Pari knew there was a chance he had been snowed by Cory. *Could he be the murderer?* Pari wondered, *Have I been played for a fool?*

Chapter 7: The Devil Can't Do It

Evelyn Valdez read through the coroner's report while she was waiting for a subdivision's CC&Rs to print. She had plenty of time to read. These Covenants, Codes and Restrictions were three hundred and seventy-nine pages. *What a waste*, she thought. *Probably no one else will ever read them.* She'd tried to get the office to go paperless, but that only went so far. Mr. Deels was all for eliminating paper, as long as it didn't get in the way of sales or legal requirements. That meant things like property listing books still had to be printed. *Reams of paper in a land with no trees*, she thought. When she had finished reading the coroner's report, she shredded it. Most people didn't realize that coroner's reports are public, but only after any police case has been decided. Evelyn had a close friend at Pima County and had learned his password habits long ago. It was a breeze for her to pull up all kinds of confidential information when she needed to do so. Still, she didn't want to get her friend in hot water, so she didn't tell him when she took a peek, and of course she never left a trail.

Most people thought she was a dumb, if lovely, secretary keeping the front desk warm. However, the agents at Deels Realty knew behind her exotic beauty was a sharp and procedural mind. It didn't bother Evelyn when people thought she was a Latina bimbo, she just used it. *Why not?* She thought. *If people can't focus on who I am that's their problem.* She had an attitude, but had a black belt in Karate to back it up.

Evelyn knew she managed Cory's business with the skill of a maestro, and in her extra time. She was there to answer the phone, of course, but that had as little to do with her real duties as her cafe con leche complexion had to do with her mind. Along with running the office, she also did property sleuthing for the boss at a handsome fee. Cory didn't mind paying because her work was always exemplary. Also, he had the added bonus of no perceived obligations to Escrow and Title companies for the research. The two of them had a mutual agreement. He gave her free access to company facilities for her personal work, and she did investigations for him; he never asked where her results came from, and she never had to tell.

Right now, Evelyn needed to have a private consult with the boss about the research she had done on the murder. After buzzing Cory to see if he was free, she made quick arrangements to visit him in his private quarters. She knew which agents were in house, because she always knew exactly where they all were. Last year she had persuaded Cory to let her put a tracking program on all the agent's smart phones. The benefit to them: deductions for taxes based on recorded mileage and always knowing where their phones were. The benefit for the Brokerage—incalculable.

Today, glancing at the screen, she saw no one present she would trust with the front desk, and no one close enough to call in, so, she announced on the intercom that she was going on break for an hour and asked Harold Wu to take a turn at the on-call desk. Once he parked himself in the glass conference room across from reception she locked up. In the back of her office was a door to the hall that stretched from the garage on the South to the North end of the building. The hall divided the Brokerage offices from the home. She took a left and passed the office supply room, then the Vault, and walked on all the way to the end of the hall. On the left was a door to Cory's office, on the right a door to his private quarters. She keyed in the combo on the right and walked down past the greenhouse to Cory Deels' bedroom and living quarters.

Cory was sitting back in his favorite chair, a dark maroon leather recliner, with his eyes closed, listening to opera. Evelyn had no great fondness for the music, but she had spent a fair amount of time learning all she could about it. Once she understood what a passion it was for Deels, she resolved to become an expert. She had even learned to appreciate Puccini. At the moment he was listening to Menotti's The Old Maid and the Thief. It was an odd choice, she thought. Generally her boss went for longer, epic operas like The Ring Cycle. Plus, he was not the greatest fan of Gian Carlo Menotti. She paused before interrupting him and looked anew at his room, the largest one on the estate. Even so, somehow Cory had managed to make it more intimate than one might expect. The walls were a hand finished soft tea stain color that bled to a golden beeswax at the edges. The room's vaulted ceiling was made up of an intricate Moroccan wood construct in octagons and stars. Rich Persian rugs were strewn on the travertine floor and his furniture was Frank Lloyd Wright inspired oak and leather modern. A fire popped on the elaborate grate of the immense fireplace, and she caught a whiff of sharp cedar smoke. Cory had a glass of tawny port sitting on the table next to a translation of Hafiz. He had a passion for Sufi ecstatic love poetry. That left her cold, she wanted her love a bit more carnal.

Without opening his eyes, he turned down the opera's volume, "What did you find out? Do they think he did it?"

"I don't believe so, but they have no other solid leads, so I guess they figured they might as well hold the one person they do have."

"That is unacceptable. What do I need to do to get him out?"

She wondered that he had not asked her if she thought Pari had committed the murder. Evelyn was uncomfortable with Pari and had thought him a liability even before the arrest. She had a hard time understanding why Cory had hired him right out of school. All the other agents in the office were experienced. That had always been Cory's business model, to pick the best, hire them away from the other brokerages and let them do their thing. *So why have you brought this greenhorn into our house?* She silently asked, then spoke to the point. "They have no right to hold him. I think you could call up a friend and make some noise...that might do it."

"Sit down, Evy. I need you after this call."

She sat on an Eams chair near the fire and watched Cory. He was a sexy if enigmatic man—hot, really. Tall, perfect Anglo skin and hair, eyes that looked directly into yours without moving away one bit—that was what really got her gut. She flushed, realizing she had been staring. So, she covered with her usual hint of contempt for the opposite sex. Most men found that irresistible, but also found themselves incapable of moving on the desire. Cory never reacted a bit; but he still kept up the air of formal intimacy no matter how much apparent contempt she turned on. So with Cory, her actions had the opposite effect, she was the one writhing with no ability to act. She looked away and then turned back and watched him dial. She was startled to hear the opera pause and the dial tone sound over the room speakers. Evelyn could not get used to the seamless way Cory had technology integrated into his life. Someone picked up on the other end.

"Hello, this is George Oldfather. How can I help you?" Evelyn hated that oily politician tone.

"George, this is Cory Deels."

"Mr. Deels, surprising to hear from you."

Irony from the Supervisor, what next? Evelyn thought.

"Indeed." Said Cory.

"What's up? How can I help?"

"Apparently Pima County has one of my agents, Pari Workingboxwalla. I understand he has been locked up without cause."

The supervisor's tone changed. "You're talking about that Arab kid who got himself involved with the murder over in Picture Rocks?"

Cory bristled. "Don't insult me, Supervisor. Oldfather. You and I both know he is nether an Arab nor the killer."

The Supervisor's voice frosted, and he upped the ante. "Well, Mr. Deels, I cannot say I know the real truth of either of your claims."

Cory sighed and put his hands together, fingers tip to tip. Evelyn knew her boss wasn't one to be cowed, so she assumed the pause was for effect.

"Don't horse shit me George. I know you have nothing to hold him on and I am asking you politely to see that he is released into my care, quid pro quo—no later than tomorrow morning."

The supervisor paused, *He's calculating the size of the favor,* Evelyn thought, *Cory had better cut the expectations down.*

The supervisor continued to bargain. "You know, I do not, strictly speaking, have anything to do with Law Enforcement. That's a different branch of government, as you know."

"You know I know more than I should know...about you and other things. Will you release him or shall we escalate this call? I believe I have the Chairperson's number on speed dial, and I have five minutes for her. That is all it should take, as you know."

George Oldfather's tone was light and friendly. "Well, I suppose I could do that, my friend. But Cory, I need your promise he won't leave the county, let alone the state."

"You have my word." The supervisor paused, but it was a bit too long to be real. Evelyn knew Cory had won.

"You can pick him up at noon tomorrow."

Evelyn could hear the anger in the abrupt hang-up at the end of the line, if not the man's voice. Cory rubbed his temples and then pushed his fingers through his long copper hair. He sat back and let out a long breath.

"Evy, I really did not want to get involved in this mess, I have many other things to do. However, I don't think we have a choice; we'll have to intervene."

She watched him turn the opera back on and wondered for a moment if she had been dismissed, then knew there was more to come.   "I would agree," she said, wondering how the involvement had changed from just him to the two of them. Still, she liked it that way.

"If you listen to the lyric playing right now Menotti says: 'The devil couldn't do what a woman can—Make a thief out of an honest man'."

"Well, Boss, you and I know Menotti is gay, so I'd say his comments are a bit suspect on the issue."

"Point taken, but the opera is really a comment on the lowest aspects of lust and greed, and those are not owned by either sex. I am thinking there may be motive here beyond what the police can see. I would like you to do a thorough history and title search on the Picture Rocks property. Also, research all the parties involved. Something is missing."

She paused, thinking about what she already knew. "Would that research include you, Mr. Deels, and Pari?" She was only partly joking.

"Don't be impertinent; I hardly need to know what my involvement entails. As far as Pari goes, it cannot hurt, though I am sure he has no real involvement. There is a motive here and it has to do with that property!"

Then he took a sip of the port and turned up the volume on the last duet in the opera. He picked up the Times and finished the last few letters in the crossword. She had been dismissed. Evelyn took the walk back in uncharacteristically deep thought. She suspected there was one little item, which if it became known could be a disaster for her boss. She did not think he could possibly be the murderer, but at the moment she supposed she could not be certain of that fact either. She resolved to do her deepest research yet. Evelyn needed to prove to herself the innocence or guilt of both men. What she would do with that knowledge she did not know, she only knew she must get to the root of the matter.

Chapter 8: Scorpion Path

Cory listened to Evelyn close the door behind her and walk back down the hall. *Damn it!* He thought, *the last thing I want is to be dragged into this mess.* Now he had to plan carefully to avoid a deluge of unwelcome publicity. *Maybe I could appeal to a certain shock jock's avarice and desire for fame*, he thought. No doubt that would be possible because he knew the fellow to be sorely lacking in the research department.

He spoke again to the air, "Music off. Call Billy Jo Zane," The system bumped the opera just before Mrs.Todd's final scene, where she discovers everything she owns has been stolen. *No loss*, he thought. It was Cory's least favorite part of the opera.

Mr. Zane's answering service picked up. "Billy Jo Zane, makes the news again! How can I help you?" the operator said.

"Hello, tell Billy Jo, that Cory Deels called. I may have some information for him of a confidential nature," *That should do it*, he thought.

"I will let Mr. Zane know. Is this the best number?"

"Yes, anytime during business hours but not Sundays."

"Thank you from the All News Channel." She hung up.

He spoke to the air again: "Music on. Brubeck, Take Five."

Cory Deels picked the Times back up, finished the Sudoku and sipped his port while he listened to the jazz. He tried not to worry over things he could not control.

Unfortunately, that wasn't working very well for him. He cut the music off with a poke at his phone. Then, abandoning the port, the book and any pretense of luxuriating in the good life, he got up.

Cory Deels was deeply disturbed. He hadn't wanted to show that emotion to Evelyn. He thought he had solidly shut down the past, but it kept cropping up in new and uncomfortable ways. He walked into the greenhouse and looked over the new crop of Boswellia. Three of the Frankincense cuttings had rooted. The sand and limestone mix was dry, so he misted them. Sadly, even his collection of rare desert plants failed to sooth him. Finding no satisfaction there, he headed out the door following the path Evelyn had taken, and continued on to the garage.

He took the Escalade, and drove through downtown, turning west, unsure of where he was going. *It's time for Mr. Deels to have a little solitude and connect with nature*, he thought. Cory found himself driving over Gates Pass and wondered at the quirky vision of Pima County. *Any municipality that bought and kept a mountain range as a park had to be admired.* Even though the air was crisp, dry and perfect for hiking, he skipped the knife-edge trail he usually took along the divide, and continued northwest. He drove through dense saguaro and cholla forests until he reached Signal Hill near the trail head to Wasson Peak. Cory studied the enigmatic Petroglyphs at Signal again. Spirals, hunted goats, snakes—today these designs seemed apt. He took off at a trot but instead of taking King's trail to the top of the Peak, he veered off to the West and found himself sitting in a familiar place, on a rock outcrop overlooking the scene of the crime. *Which crime am I here for?* He wondered.

Below him the desert looked incredibly lush. This year's monsoon had been ample and the saguaros were fat and healthy, their silvery needles glowed to gold in the last rays of the October evening. To the North, the cliffs of Picture Rocks shown vermilion, followed by magenta and then winked to indigo as the sun passed below the horizon. Cory stayed still, until Polaris twinkled above him to the North. The sky deepened to black velvet, a color usually seen only on dry November nights deep in the desert. Despite the city on the other side of the Tucson Mountains, the stars were brilliant and manifested the true Milky Way: a parade of stars that shamed any city glow. Night grew chilly and Cory shivered as he watched the lights wink on and off in sequence though the home on Scorpion Path: Woodrow Madrone's home.

Who is with Woody? He wondered, noting the Humvee in the driveway. He had owned this house before Woody. It was Cory's first home, also home to his failed marriage, a broken partnership and the birth of his son—an ill fated home. Now it was also a house of murder. What he couldn't figure out was why no one had arrived with a warrant for Madrone, or why they hadn't taken him in right away for that matter. *Can no one else see the man had motive and plenty of opportunity?* He wondered. *Perhaps they simply assumed it was Pari through prejudice—fear of the unknown dark skinned Indian who was there at the scene.*

Still, Cory knew that despite his youth and innocence, Pari had had some unsavory dealings with the victim, *What a pickle,* he thought. Cory was just about to leave when the front door opened and a man stepped out. Cory muttered aloud in surprise: "Why, George Oldfather, what are you doing here?" Then, realizing what he had done, he held his breath. The county supervisor turned abruptly and looked in his direction. Cory froze remembering with chagrin how easily sound carried in the desert. Apparently he had not been spotted, because Oldfather turned back to the doorway and spoke to the man just emerging from the house.

"A moment! Wait, stay there." He looked back into the night, searching. Cory realized George was probably blinded by the porch light. The darkness of the desert might just save him from discovery.

"Dios mio! What is wrong?" said Madrone, coming out on the stoop.

"Maybe a coyote. I thought I heard something. I think I'm sure no one is out there." Woody looked into the desert as well before handing the supervisor a package.

"Mira, here it is, take it. I want this shit out of my home."

"Is this all of it? Got her pipes, spoons and needles? We can't have anything left here that might link her to me."

"That is everything, eso es todo, and good riddance. We got to cool this shit, campadre."

Even from a distance Cory could see that Oldfather stiffened, no doubt hating the familiarity.

"Of course, Señor" Oldfather said with his terrible accent, "we are done, for the time being."

"Bueno. Madre, I wish she hadn't died, but I am glad to be done with this problem. You said your guy was sure that boy shot her."

"He said so, but now I am sure he didn't. I'm not sure you didn't shoot her though. Just don't tell me if you did."

"Estupido. I am many things but I would not kill such a pathetic soul."

"Whatever. I can't keep Deels' agent in jail any longer though. I'm already getting pressure."

"You should keep him."

"The idiot didn't fire his gun at her. You saw him hit the floor. He only fired one bullet. The kid was bloody from trying to help. I can't hold him. You'd better keep quiet about all this."

"No me jodas! You have fucked this up. Son of a bitch, cabron! Get out!" With that, Woody slammed the door and George Oldfather got in his Humvee and left.

Cory sat there for a few minutes digesting this new information. *Drugs? That is big news indeed if a supervisor is involved*. George Oldfather was the last hope of an old Southern Arizonan family, and he had aspirations for higher office running on the family reputation. Cory thought the Supervisor might have fallen far from the family tree's roots.

☼

Unknown to Cory, another pair of eyes had been watching the exchange below. Carole Anne Michaels, ex wife of both Cory Deels and Woody Madrone sat back on her haunches. She'd stalked Cory with great stealth and tiptoed along a ridge of exposed rock in her tennies. She knew she hadn't made a sound. She'd walked this path before, many times, could walk it blindfolded. She used to hunt the valley and had an uncanny trail sense. Carole Anne knew the slopes of Wasson peak better than anyone. She took a long, slow breath in and opened her senses. The air was thick with the iodine smell of creosote bush.

Even so, Carol Anne could smell the skunky odor of a javolina herd near by, mixed in with Cory's Bayberry scent. She'd often wondered why he stuck with that old-fashioned cologne. It made her want to puke, always had. She didn't know any woman who would put up with it, if she had a choice. Of course most women she knew had no choice. *We have to put up with much worse than that just to survive*, she thought. She listened for the small animals and flicked a scorpion away. She played with the idea of surprising Cory in the bush. *I'd give him a heart attack!* She almost laughed out loud, and then realized the best course was to wait for the self-righteous prick to leave.

She watched him get up and head back to his SUV. *Good riddance*. She sighed, glad she had waited him out. She knew his limits and hers. Her tab with him was tapped out, had been for quite a while. Carole Anne thought back to the first days she had lived here...stuck, no transportation and, pregnant. The only person she could get to visit her out here then was her friend Dolores Samaniego. She sighed again, sad for their ruined friendship—not all her fault, *but still, you can't make old friends*, she mused. Nevertheless, she suspected Dolores might have been in on something here too. Why else would she have been here on that awful, fateful day?

She got up and started back on the long trail to her Harley. *Might as well head into Marana,* she thought. There wasn't much point in her staying here. She knew Woody had locked the house up tight, so there was no way to try to find what she needed now, even if it was here. No way she wanted to see him either. Too much history and too much to lose....and no way for her to take any revenge for the mess that had happened in the house below—a house she knew better than any other, a house of love and shame. Scorpion Path, a home she couldn't let go of, a place that stung her in the heart.

She needed a drink, or a line—something to take away the ache and fill the void. Sadness threatened to smother her. Carole Anne couldn't bear enclosures of any sort, especially emotional confinement. She thought she might head to a bar, or find a one night companion somewhere else—anywhere else but here. She decided instead to drive. She kicked the Harley alive and headed west. Wind buffeting her chest and the thrum of the motor between her thighs were caress enough for the night.

Chapter 9: Jailed

Pari opened his eyes in fear and panic, sore as hell. His shoulders and hips were aching from sleeping on the slab. *Where am I?* He thought, totally disoriented from sleep. *I don't recognize anything—is it the beach?* The window was barred and dark. *Breathe, center, focus....Slow down*, he thought. Out of nowhere he heard his mother calling. "Pari." His clothes were damp. Confused, he ran out the door and found himself on the street.

He was frightened and lost. The street was chaotic—heavy traffic and people, lots of people shouting. He didn't know what was going on. A truck honked and braked, nearly hitting him. A couple of old men riding bikes were laughing. He stepped into a hole and his shoe was soaked with muddy sewage water. The fetid stink was mixed with the scent of roses and frying onions, cloying and unsettling. A man, his lips stained blood red with beetle juice, sat amid piles of brightly colored pigment. He grabbed a handful of dye and threw it at Pari. The tint was as red as the old fellow's teeth. He disappeared in a magenta nimbus.

The color stuck to Pari's shirt and damp pants, looking like a target or an arrow. *Which?* He shook the muck off his foot. He tried to find his direction but his mother was still shouting: "Pari-jan." Her voice irritated him. Now Pari could see he was mistaken; the man was actually a girl. She offered him tea. He took the cup and sat to sip, but he spilled it. The girl's stiff sari was gold, or green, he could not decide which. He stood, mumbling, stumbling, spilling the tea again. Like blotter ink, it spread, it was bright, a red tincture. The scent of copper and rust sickened him, he was afraid he would vomit. He looked over to see the girl splayed on the ground. She was bleeding out, but she smiled at him.

I can't breathe, why can't I breathe? Who is she? She mumbled his name and then died. *She's dead*, he thought, *it's my fault, my fault!*

Pari woke up in his cell, crying.

His shoulders and hips still ached from the slab, but the worst pain was what he was feeling: guilt and dread. His heart was filled with loneliness and sadness. He wished he were still asleep— even the nightmare was better than these heavy feelings. He was wide awake now, and still in jail, but his terrible dream broke a dam. As his tears began to flow, he realized he was not just crying for Dory, he was crying for himself. *Could I have changed the outcome?* He wondered, *I think I could have—I wish I had.*

Pari stared the old, pale green walls of his cell, walls scratched and marked with the messages of past residents. He felt now that he belonged here, and as he read those communications, one struck him in the heart. Amid all the names, the rude pictures of dicks, cunts and asses, the scratched-in faces and cuss words, centered in this crude graffiti was a message: "Fucker! You used her, you abused her, and now you're lost, you perfect asshole." It could not have been more personal if she had said it to him.

Sitting in that jail cell, racked with guilt, he had no one to blame but himself. *I was rude and short with Dory when what she really needed was a friend. I blamed her, but it was my responsibility,* he thought, *I am the perfect asshole.* Unfortunately, it was too late to take anything back and his hindsight counted for less than nothing. Now, remembering that frail body pumping out the last of its blood, he began to cry for what he felt was his part in her murder, for his lack of responsibility.

Chapter 10: Through the Mirror

Officer Philip Moreno watched Pari through the two-way mirror. He knew the young man had something to do with the mess at the Picture Rocks house, but he could not decide what. He was sure it wasn't murder, but he knew this fellow was involved in more ways than he was letting on. Moreno knew the look of guilt. Besides, there were too many coincidences: the kid's fingerprints at last year's bust, the robbery, the fact that Workingboxwalla found the body—too many coincidences to be chance. Moreno did not believe in coincidence.

At that bust he had apprehended Dorothea Samaneigo trying to buy cocaine at the crack house over on Freemont. They'd shut it down the night before, but he'd decided to run a sting the next day to pick up any suppliers and users who might drop by before the word got out. He'd let her go, after finding nothing—even though it was obvious she was stoned and looking for junk. He could see she'd been up all night and now he supposed it must have been with this guy, Philip had a soft spot for the Samaneigo family, since they'd had so much loss. He was the officer who had notified Dolores Samaniego, the girl's mom about her daughter Mary dying from an overdose. He heard later that the Hernan, the girl's father, had completely broken down—he died later in the year. Yet, Dolores had just stood there, stoic, without a tear, and asked where the other girl was. *The other girl*. He couldn't get over the way she put it, "Where is the other girl?"

Moreno had given Dory stern warnings, even before that day, not wanting to bust her. He even kept her distracted while his cohorts did their business during the bust, so she wouldn't further incriminate herself. His officers dusted the jeep and later ran the prints through IAFIS, the FBI fingerprint database. He'd found fingerprints, but didn't know they were Pari's since at that point his weren't in the database.

Then, last week, Moreno had gone out to Picture Rocks to investigate a robbery called in by a real estate agent. Surprise, it was Pari Workingboxwalla. In Arizona, all real estate agents are fingerprinted before being issued a license. Officer Moreno had access to that database. The prints that turned up at the scene belonged to Madrone, Workingboxwalla and the Samaniego girl. When he followed up, Woody Madrone told him the girl was living there from time to time, and Pari was showing the house, so....It sounded like another dead end, except Moreno thought it might be an inside job. Users needed money, and he knew Pari's prints had been the ones on the Jeep the day of the bust—too coincidental.

Now the word had come down from on high to let him go. Why would Oldfather intervene? Normally he would have resisted the push from the supervisor as inappropriate, but in this case Philip thought he might learn more by playing along. Perhaps a brief conversation with Mr. Deels would help.

Philip had known Cory for quite a few years. *Hell*, he thought, *who doesn't know Cory Deels?* It seemed to Philip, that Cory knew half the city. He figured the other half knew Cory's face and name from all the advertising. The real question for Philip was, where to have the conversation. He believed a talk here at the jail might not yield any substantial information. His radio buzzed and the officer in charge told him it was time to release Workingboxwalla, that Deels was there to pick him up. *Perhaps this is a chance to set up a meeting.* Moreno walked to the front and stuck his hand out.

"Cory, how have you been? What are you doing over here on my side of town?"

"Philip, good to see you. I am just fine, thanks. Since I am quite sure you know why I am here, I will dispense with the answer to your second question. However, why have you come out to see me?"

Moreno decided to cut through the bull and just state his case. "All right. I don't think your young man murdered the Samaniego girl, but his hands are messy enough, I think someone over at the DA's might try a circumstantial case anyway, if nothing else shows up."

"I was not aware you had a thing on him."

"We don't, really. However, Pari knew her, and more intimately than some might guess. I'm just suggesting it might be in our mutual interest to finally have that dinner you promised me so long ago."

Cory paused and Philip could see there was a mutual interest. "Philip, you know you are always welcome at my table. Besides, I am quite sure Evelyn would love to see you." Moreno flushed, and wondered how much Deels knew. Cory laughed, "Don't worry, Evy never kisses and tells. I have other sources. Yes, a dinner would be good, perhaps we could pool our information."

"Okay, great, let me know when." With that Moreno retreated wondering who would end up the wiser after the dinner.

☼

Cory almost laughed as Officer Moreno left the room, but he held his amusement inside. The man was earnest and meant well, which was more than Cory could say about many in his profession.

Right now though, he knew his efforts needed to be redoubled, starting with a frank conversation with Pari.

Just then they let his agent out of holding and gave Pari his possessions in an envelope. Pari was about to speak, but Cory put a finger to his lips and led the way out the door and to the SUV. Once they were inside, he gave a voice command to the blue-tooth sound system, to make sure there was no conversation till he was ready. "Play, Faiz Ali Faiz." The Sufi qawwali began to sing. Cory knew Pari found the music peculiar. He'd chosen this music to keep Pari quiet while they drove. It seemed to work. He could sense Pari trying to put his thoughts together. Cory knew the ten minutes of the current song would about get them up to the top of Sentinel Peak and give Pari time he needed to compose himself.

The drive up Sentinel Peak, or A Mountain as most called it, took a minute less than Cory had guessed, but it was pleasant. The late October air was cool without being brisk and exceedingly clear. It was one of those days of stunning clarity, with a visibility of 80 miles or more. Cory looked out over the valley spread out before them, surrounded by mountains: this was basin and range geography. Twenty-five miles to the East, the Rincon Mountains rose blue and massive, 20 miles to the Northeast, the Catalinas punched the sky at 10,000 feet, even more majestic. Almost 40 miles to the Southeast, the Santa Rita's poked up and framed the basin that held the city. Mount Wrightson, looking like a South Western Mt. Fuji, was the highest peak in that range, taller than the Catalinas. Cory parked at the top of Sentinel peak, at a modest 2,897 feet, the outlying flank of the Tucson Mountains. Below them, in the valley lay the city. The promontory of this old volcanic range hemmed in Tucson on the West. *All this grandeur and yet we pay it no attention.*

Cory thought. The music finished and he turned off the engine. They sat there in silence for a few moments and then Pari began to speak.

"I didn't do it. I didn't kill her."

"Of course you didn't, but you did something, and I need to know exactly what—if *I* am to protect you, if I am to protect us both. Are you aware that I am legally responsible for you?"

Pari looked surprised. "Sir?"

"You were acting as my agent when you found that girl. Oh yes, the things you do affect all sorts of people. You do nothing alone. This is to say nothing of the gun you took from my son's room. What were you thinking?"

"I'm sorry, Cory."

Deels looked at the young fellow, still not quite a man. Pari looked ready to cry, but rather than irritating him, as it would have with most men, he felt protective.

"I need you to tell me the whole story, everything you did with the Samaniego girl, up until and including the day of the murder."

Pari began to speak, and as he told his tale, Cory sat back, closed his eyes and listened, taking it all in. He realized that he had become very fond of this young man and that, whatever his involvement, he would stand by him. The story was long and involved and Cory could see why Officer Moreno thought a prosecutor might want to take his agent to court. After Pari had finished the tale, Cory pressed the ignition button and started back down the mountain, taking the short route back home.

He knew Pari was waiting for a word from him, insecure about their relationship. In many ways they barely knew each other. *Still, the boy has no one else to help him*, he thought. *It is a cold and lonely world if we do not value those who are near us. I hope he had the courage to tell me everything.* He also wondered if he was filling an empty place left in his heart by the broken relationship with his son with Pari. *Perhaps he fills a more primal void,* he reflected. *It is enough to be glad of the companionship and company.* Then he turned his attention back to the young man.

"How much of this did you tell the police?" Cory asked, clearly on Pari's side.

"Almost all of it. I told them about the first time I did drugs with Dory, but not about the sex. And I didn't tell them about the second time or about finding her at the robbery."

"Why did you tell them something but not everything?"

"Well, they knew I had been with her the first time, I guess they'd found my prints when they arrested her the next day. But they didn't know anything else and I really didn't want..."

"Yes, I get it. Unfortunately you're already on the list, and it is very hard to get off that page."

"Also, I was...am, embarrassed about the sex, and I was trying to protect her. I was sure she didn't rob the house."

"Why?"

"She said she lived there. Why would she rob her own house?"

"That is not her house, it is Woodrow Madrone's home, I should know."

"She said she had title to it."

"What?" He stopped the car then and pulled over to the curb. "You didn't mention that to me earlier. Are you sure she said that?"

"Yes, but I thought she was just giving me a line, and I didn't think it was important. I figured she had some arrangement with Mr. Madrone"

Cory thought this over. "Not impossible, but unlikely. I know Woody. Never mind. Did you mention the business about the title to anyone else? To your clients?"

"No, why would I?"

Cory brought the car back into traffic. "Because, my young apprentice, matters of ownership are material to a sale. If your clients want to live in this property, they have to buy that right from the person who owns it. If somehow she held title, then the complete ownership is not Woodrow Madrone's. Enough of this for now. I need your help. Tonight is Halloween and there are preparations to be finished. The pasadizo needs to be decorated and someone must sit behind the gate to watch for children, work the effects and hand out the candy. That shall be you. While you are waiting for them I want you to really use your journal. You need...no, we need a strict accounting of everything. Include every detail of what you told me and anything else you remember. Anything at all having to do with this situation, up until we met today."

     With that, he turned from 18th into the garage and parked. After exiting the vehicle, Cory opened a storage locker devoted to holiday decorations. He pointed to the shelves housing the Halloween collection and handed Pari his concise instructions for placement, assembly and operation. His mind was already working through the minutia of Pari's story, sifting the details to find anything that could give them an advantage. It was a skill he used to good effect in contract negotiations. He knew it also made him seem aloof and cold, but without a word, Cory took the door to the passageway to his rooms, leaving Pari to fend for himself.

Chapter 11 The Journal

Pari made a quick meal of olives, cheese and roasted eggplant on a baguette, gathered several boxes of Halloween decorations from the garage and made his way to the pasadizo. He opened the first box and read the enumerated instructions. Cory is nothing if not detail oriented, he thought. He found stuff for both the front of the house and the pasadizo—webs, skulls and bones, cauldrons of bubbling fog and a light and sound show. Pari knew the other barrio residents thought Cory's house was an exercise in conspicuous consumption, but Cory had told him they always brought their kids by for the show. It took Pari quite a while to set up the elaborate Halloween diorama, but once he had finished, he took a seat on the side and began to write.

I've got to get the past down. Cory's right, things begin to blur with time. Even the simplest memories fall into doubt. The past is never what anyone recalls. I think we unconsciously change the past to fit what we already believe. Whenever I have gone on a hunt for evidence to support my beliefs, I've found the proof, whether the evidence really exists or not. So, since I don't remember my past without a bias, I must record it. Otherwise, other people's bias may later win the day. I wonder though—if every person's past is unique, where is the truth?

He looked at this beginning with some doubt, unsure if he was taking the right tone. *Also, who exactly am I addressing?* He wondered. Then he realized he'd forgotten to light the oil lamps in the pasadizo. Pari had just finished that task when the first visitors arrived. It was still early, the sun only beginning to set, but he knew that was when parents brought their infants. He welcomed a mother with two toddlers dressed as Dora the Explorer and Scooby-do. Mom was wowed, but he overdid the effects, scaring the kids when he hit the fog and the scream buttons. *Those two wailed louder than the banshee over the speakers*, he thought. Their mother gave him a sour look as he apologetically loaded their bags with candy.

Once they left, Cory's voice boomed out over the sound system, "Pari, save the special effects for the teenagers. I don't want to get sued for child abuse."

"Sorry Cory," he said. Seeing no more visitors, he sat down on one of the benches in the pasadizo to get back to the journal. Trying to narrow the focus a bit, he decided to begin with the second time he had met Dory.

After that disastrous first night with Dory, I went back to school, much as I hated it. Whenever our intern journal nights came up, of course, I faithfully attended. I see now, part of that was because I hoped I would see Dory there again. Hope and fear tied together is a dangerous combination for me. I didn't see her, and that only made my craving stronger. The next time Dory and I met was after I returned from my trip to India...after quitting med-school and getting my Real Estate License.

After filling in the details of his meeting with Spike, a group of children approached the house and he stopped writing. These kids were a bit older, he saw, perhaps first graders. He was more judicious and gave them a little fog but held off on the screams. They oohed and ahed over the fog, but the candy was the big hit. Cory's candy, like all his food, is the best and Pari had been instructed to give it in quantity. He went back to his journal including how his relationship with Cory began, on the chance this document became a court record.

Pari set the journal down again as the next group of kids arrived. This time he entertained a teenage boy and girl bringing their ten-year-old brother and his three friends. He used the scream button as well as the fog. As the kids came forward for the candy, Pari stepped on the light show button. Cory has a laser projector programmed to zap the fog where it came out. Anyone standing in the center of the pasadizo can see the illusion of a couple of ghosts coming out of the walls. The older boy startled, dropped his candy and shrieked. Pari felt bad but joined the rest of the group in laughter. Finally, after a little embarrassment, the boy also laughed. Pari stepped on the button again and like clockwork they all screamed and laughed together. They thanked him and headed down the street. Pari could see no one else on the way, so he picked the journal back up.

He had a hard time writing again after describing his encounter with Spike. *I'm not gay!* He thought, knowing in his heart that the jury was out on that question. Nevertheless, he knew he needed to finish recording all that had happened, if he was to establish his innocence in the murder.

I don't remember if we had sex or not. I know that sounds silly but in a way it doesn't matter. If we didn't I would have wanted to try it out, and what I can recall might as well have been the whole thing. I was too stoned to remember—we could have, but I don't think we did. Am I reinventing the past? Perhaps, but whatever we did is not relevant to Dory's death. That is the point, isn't it?

Page 66

The very next time I met Dory requires more background ... it was at the theft, but to make sense of it and why I was there, I have to fill in some details. Even after I quit med school I still hung out with my old crowd, though I never saw Dory there again. I heard she started using meth, and that broke my heart. I don't really think I could have done anything about that, but I didn't try. Spike showed up a couple of times, coming with one intern or another. I pretended as though we barely knew each other and that made me nervous even though he was great about it. Once he showed up with an openly gay doctor. I was jealous and I barely acknowledged the two of them. I see now I was afraid to be grouped in with them, called a fag. He nodded to me, was friendly, but discrete and made no fuss, but even that made me feel like crap. I was, no, I am a hypocrite and a coward. The thing is, I still don't know myself if I am gay or if that whole thing was just the cocaine and the moment. Plenty of guys have done stuff. Yeah, I know, too much protesting. Point is: I don't know.

Pari was glad to see another group of kids come in. This time he got into the smoke and mirrors, forgetting for a while all the questions he had been pondering. The kids were older too, so he ran the routine from the library, the small room to the north of the pasadizo. The door to that room opens with an electronic key, in combination with a touch on one of the iron figurines that stand in front of the sconces. He knew Cory was serious about security since Woody's break-in. The kids wandered into the pasadizo looking for someone to give them candy, Pari could tell they were scared but trying not to show it. When they were safely in the breezeway Pari slammed the gate shut. He made the screams, fog and light show erupt and then he showered them with little bags of candy. He didn't open the gate till they picked the candy up. Pari thought it very cool. After they left, he saw the block was clear and he went back to the journal.

At one journal session, a couple of my friends mentioned they were ready to look for a house. Dana and Rupert Brooks, my first clients. Finding them a house led me to this mess.

That evening, just JP, Elsie, Rupert and Dana Brooks, Spike and I were at the journal session. JP had just finished his journal entry for the week when his partner, Elise, asked me what work I was doing now. Everyone knew I had quit medicine but no one had asked why. It seems a little lame now, but I decided to launch into a speech on my new profession, with a dose of self-parody to cover my insecurity.

"I've decided to specialize in those patients who want to find a house and need my guidance to thread the intricate maze leading to home ownership!"

Elsie gave an uncertain laugh. "What, you're selling houses?"

"No, I am a fiduciary agent, a REALTOR. I've passed my state Boards and now have my license to practice with Deels Realty. I'm not a salesperson, I'm an adviser." It fell flat. I was anxious, and wondered if I would hear some tired joke about used car salespeople. It was awkward. I figured my only hope was utter

sincerity. After all, these were my friends. "Gang, I'm really happy I took this route. I knew medicine wasn't for me last year and a few of you knew that too." Murmurs of agreement encouraged me. "What surprised me is how pleased and happy I am to be doing this." I wondered if I was a bit too earnest for this crowd, but got a pleasant surprise instead.

Rupert spoke up, with real excitement. "Man, that is great, Pari! Dana and I just decided to buy a house and we were wondering who we could use to help us! We need someone we can trust, who will listen to what we need. I think that is you."

I was thrilled, but would never have guessed that this first sale would involve a journey to jail. Dana, Rupert and I set up our first meeting for the following day. They gave me a list of homes they had already found on the net, and one in particular they wanted to see right away, the house on Scorpion Path. How fast and sure the noose tightened!

I didn't realize at the time the house was Mr. Madrone's. I should have done my research. I should have looked up past sales and tax records. I also should have asked my broker to talk to me again about first steps. I was new, very green and embarrassed to show my ignorance. I didn't realize I had an obligation to perform due diligence for my clients before a showing. I didn't know that was the house where Dory lived. Excuses. I just called the number to set up the showing and a strange but vaguely familiar voice set up the time and gave me the alarm codes. It didn't occur to me to think about who that might have been.

Pari took a break again and, though there were no children, he ran the machines and took a bag of candy from the pot. He ate it with more than a little guilt, expecting to hear Cory's voice admonishing him. He scarfed down the Godiva truffles in silence, wishing for something more familiar. A piece of candy corn would have been just fine. Again, he went back to the pen.

We drove up Ina Road and over the pass at Picture Rocks. It's a great drive and we were soon lost in conversation. Then, just after we passed the edge of Saguaro National Monument West, the owner called me and asked if I had forgotten the code. I laughed.

"I don't think so. Why? We haven't been there yet."

"Extraño" he said, "I just got a call from the police. The last agent must have neglected to turn it back on after showing. Please reset it when you go. Comprende?" Again, that familiar voice, and Spanish...I should have known.

"Sure." I said.

When we arrived the siren had shut off. I assumed that was automatic or someone had just turned it off and reset it. I got the key from the lock-box and opened the door. My clients rushed in to go look at the magnificent living room and the high wall of glass that let in the magnificent view of the desert flanking Wasson Peak. Dana was telling Rupert to come see the kitchen, built around a giant boulder. Rupert had already found the extravagant atrium in the center of the house, a kind of greenhouse packed with tropical plants and exotic birds, fully walled and roofed in glass. The living room, kitchen, dining room and master bedroom each connected to it. The plantings and landscape features inside were so dense you could not see from one room to the other. I had to sign in and turn off the alarm system in the entry hall when I saw the damage.

The security system lay on the floor, and the wall where it had been mounted showed where the screws had pulled from the sheetrock. I saw someone flit between the study and the master bedroom. It didn't even occur to me that it might be a robbery or a home invasion. I just figured the owner was still here. Stupidly, I assumed the security system had somehow fallen off the wall. So I said, "Hello" and stepped into the Master—I was shocked to see Dory with a wad of paper and jewelry in her hands. She was trying to get out the window in the master bathroom, but it was very small and she had to drop the loot first.

"Dory, what's going on?"

Startled, she wheeled around, then whispered."Shit, Workingboxwalla, what the fuck are you doing here?"

"I'm showing the house, what are you doing here?"

"I live here you idiot, or I used to. I was...I was just coming back for some things."

"Where's your jeep?"

"In the shop, I've got a ride coming." I must have looked doubtful; she was extremely nervous. I thought she might be "Jonesing" and needed a fix. She spoke again,"Look, I have to go. I'm leaving all this stuff, even though its mine—none of it matters. Swear to me you won't say anything." She dropped everything except for a paper she stuck in her back pocket; she saw me watching her. "It's nothing, just a, a note really, from my mom, from my real mom."

"Dory, the police are on their way, the alarm..."

"Swear you won't tell, you owe me that. Swear!"

So I promised Dorothea Samaniego I would not tell about the day she tried to rob her own home. How I wish I had not kept that promise.

Another bunch of Kids arrived, so Pari put the book down again, he was getting tired of the Halloween routine, but these kids grabbed their candy and were gone in a moment.

So the police came, Officer Moreno if you can believe it, though I didn't know him then. My clients saw and knew nothing, and I said as much about it myself. Despite the excitement we finished touring the house and they decided they wanted to make an offer. I was surprised, given the attempted robbery, but I certainly didn't object. It would be my first sale, after all.

Rupert told his wife, "You can have a theft anywhere. The security system worked, nothing was taken."

True, nothing was really taken that day, nothing that didn't belong to Dory. The loss came later.

The next day I got a letter from Dory, an apology. I'd opened it thinking it would be a plea for cash and was ashamed to think that when I found nothing of the sort. On the contrary, it was sincere and heartfelt. She had enclosed another envelope, a bit smaller. On the outside she'd printed "Do not open until your birthday, on pain of early death." Typical Dory humor. I filed it away as requested as my birthday was not till February. In the letter she thanked me for our friendship and told me she loved me—like a brother. Also, she apologized for introducing me to drugs. It touched me, but thinking on it now the tone was extremely final, as if she knew we wouldn't see one another again.

Rupert and Dana settled on their offer, and looking up the tax records before writing it I learned the house belonged to Mr. Madrone. I also saw that Cory had owned it before him. In my rush to get the offer in, I assumed he had owned many houses. I thought that if my offer was accepted, I could ask Cory about the house then and crow about selling "his house." I didn't want to bother him or kill the sale, remembering the argument he'd had with Mr. Madrone. Also, I really wanted to do the whole thing on my own, to prove myself. I should have informed my clients and my broker of everything relevant to the sale. So much for hindsight. No excuse, but I was green and I didn't think it was a big deal.

My clients had just graduated and were doctors making plenty of money. Rupert had some family money as well and decided to pay cash. Since the house was priced right we agreed right away. I scheduled inspections for the next day.

I pulled up to the house early and looked around the front before going in. All the excitement of the previous visit had made me nervous. I'd heard stories about agents having violent confrontations at vacant houses. This time I was alone, and the house is really isolated, so I'd taken the precaution of bringing a gun I'd found in a drawer in Cory's son's room. The inspector was due in a few minutes, but Rupert and Dana were to arrive a little later, after he had thoroughly checked the house out.

I opened the front door never thinking that the alarm would have been repaired and the code changed. It beeped and I tried pushing in the code I could remember. Nothing worked—then I heard a sound I couldn't identify, like a firecracker, then another. I heard someone open and close a door in the back of the house. Too much was happening all at once.

A sudden blaring, screeching siren sounded, followed by another noise—a noise I knew to be a shot. I heard breaking glass, more doors slamming, then running footsteps, I started to leave the house but as I turned toward the door another shot rang out and a scream came from the atrium. I don't know how many shots there were but the scream scared me. Without thinking, I pulled the gun from my belt.

I ran to the glass door into the Atrium, off the living room, where I'd heard the scream. Then another door opened and closed. I came around the corner just a moment before Mr. Madrone entered from the door to the dining room. He was also carrying a gun. In a moment of terror I pulled the trigger before even raising the gun and a panel of glass shattered and fell. I dropped the gun, horrified at what I saw in front of me. Madrone shot automatically but managed to pull his gun up just enough to miss me, realizing I was not the threat. Another avalanche of glass. Then he saw her too. There, on the floor, lying in a pool of her own blood was Dorothea Samaniego. Her face was white, but she was still alive. Mr. Madrone cried out, and fell to his knees. I did everything I knew to stop the bleeding and keep her breathing. Air was sucking in and frothy blood was coming out of a hole in her chest. Her lips were blue and a little stream of blood bubbled from the corner of her mouth. I tore her blouse to expose the wound and plugged it with a finger, but there was a larger exit wound in her back. I tried to get to that but I knew I was already too late. I called out "Dory!"

She opened her eyes, smiled and said "Workingboxwalla, good name."

Then she died.

Chapter 12: The Real Deal

Evelyn wrote Philip a quick note and left it next to his wallet on the nightstand. She watched him sleep as she pulled on her stockings and got ready for the day. He was a handsome man with his red curly hair and freckles. *Irish genes and Mexican culture...the best of both worlds*, she thought. While she felt he wasn't the brightest light in the heavens; she knew he was smart enough, honest, true and a very tender lover. *That's what really matters. Anyway, I prefer to be the brains. So why do I run away whenever we get close? Perhaps he's too good, too solid. Perhaps he doesn't challenge me.* Deep in her heart, though, she knew the real reason was that he gave her too much attention. Evy wanted to chase, not be pursued. Doting attention and moon eyes just pissed her off.

She jumped into her red Boxer and left rubber on the drive as she pealed out from home. She smiled, turned on the radio and began the 45-minute drive to work with pleasure. She loved her house. Cory had found her a real deal on a foreclosure almost all the way to Baboquivari, near the reservation. This suited her mother over in Sells just fine but made her friends in town nuts. "We have to pack a lunch to visit," they'd say, "Then pack one and stay the night" she always told them. It didn't matter to her if they never visited. This home gave her the two things she really needed, privacy and a long drive to almost anywhere. Most people thought that was strange, but her car was her one real indulgence. Any chance she got to use it, she took. Driving was a vacation to Evelyn.

A commercial over the radio squawked, voiced over by Billy Jo Zane. "Looking for the real deal on a short sale or a foreclosure? Look no further than Deels Realty. He's the man with a plan and the guiding hand who always says yes I can. Call 1-800-BUY-DEEL"

"So cheesy," she thought, but she knew it worked. Zane's voice came back on the box.

"What prominent County Supervisor seems to be living a little too high on the hog? Could it be a certain old fatherly type who will soon be up for reelection? Let me have an Amen to that! My question is: how can he afford that expensive new Humvee on a supervisor's salary? Stay tuned for a little speculation, brothers and sisters. Billy Jo Zane is planning on bringing our big spender a Come to Jesus moment real soon now, ya hear?"

Evelyn snapped off the radio with annoyance. *How did that two bit mouth get ahold of my info?* She wondered, swerving a bit to miss a coyote.

Evy hated having her thunder stolen. She turned east onto Ajo Road and stepped on the gas—no scenic routes this morning. She'd head straight to the freeway and on to the office. She wanted to get there before Cory made an appearance.

☼

Philip hadn't really been completely asleep. He loved the feeling of having a partner and wished it were Evelyn. He dreamed of waking up in the morning with her and sharing life, so he wanted these moments to last a little longer than they ever did. He knew from experience that the moment he woke up she'd get chilly and leave. It was really better to let her do her own thing in the morning. The best way for him to do that was to feign sleep. After he heard her spin out, he hopped out of bed and poured the coffee she had left in the pot, looking over the note and the paper. The note was the usual: "Bye, got to get into work early. Didn't want to wake you, hugs—E".

A Deed After Death   The Real Deal

He turned to the newspaper, what was left of it. Evelyn destroyed the news—folding, curling, scribbling on it. She always did the puzzles in ink, but rarely got the right answer the first time. Last, she ripped out the pages and articles she wanted to review. He loved cleaning up the mess she left in the mornings. He just wished he could figure out how to make it permanent. *How can I win her? Can I? Is it possible?* He wondered. He noticed an article about the Samaniego murder had been partially torn out. He decided she didn't want him to know she was looking into it. *Probably trying to protect Deels*, he thought, with more than a little jealousy.

Moreno thought through the suspect list while he sat there, admitting to himself that he was stuck. He kept hoping to narrow the field of suspects but it kept growing.

- Pari Workingboxwalla (still not off the list)

- Terry Smith, AKA "Spike" (just came to his attention, a drug pusher involved with Pari and both Samaniego girls)

- Woody Madrone (Madrone thought he was clear but it turns out he had some unsavory relationship with the deceased)

- Carole Anne Michaels (who was overheard shouting at Dory and her pusher, Spike, while presumably buying a little cocaine)

- Cory Deels (unlikely but possible...just because).

- Dolores Samaniego (he understood there had been an argument between Dory and Dolores the day before)

Page 78

Apparently the argument concerned the reason Dory had ended up at Woody Madrone's house. He figured he might need to talk to Dolores again. He'd been the one to tell her about Dory's death. She was tough though and had diverted the conversation. Then she lit into him about Mary, her other dead daughter. He wasn't looking forward to another confrontation. Perhaps he'd put that off and spend the day looking into Spike.

☼

This morning Spike was just getting home from his second job, delivering papers. *Pain in the ass career path,* he thought, *but it pays the rest of the rent*. Between that and his night shift, cleaning at the University Medical Center, he made enough to get by but never enough to pay all the bills, so he had supplemented with a little extra cash by supplying drugs here and there. He thought about how far he'd come from the naïve Terry Smith he'd been in Salina Kansas only two years before at the beginning of summer basketball camp. He'd been a good enough player to get himself on a small scholarship, but not good enough to play first bench, and too short to demand a place on the court and off the bench.

At the end of the first season the coach had caught him smoking a bit of weed—not his first offense—and that was it. He was really ready to leave the team anyway. Most people his first year there had thought he was a Mormon: the way he dressed, his name and the neat, short hair.

He'd decided a makeover was in order, and he'd made his way to Tucson—a big change from Kansas. He took up four-wheeling and caving, both new adventures, and had met the Samaniego sisters in the process. They were a little wilder than he was, but not by too much. He'd ended up sleeping with Mary, or trying to. Mary had helped him figure out that he was bi, even though she wasn't interested in that scene. *Great girl*, he thought, wistfully. At the time she'd been playing around with the Goth look, so he'd gotten into leather too, grew his hair out, got a few tattoos, and changed his name to fit the person he'd become. Spike. It seemed to suit him, so he kept it. By that time he'd become involved in dealing.

The hospital job had come with unexpected side benefits. Some of the docs liked a little snort occasionally. They could pay and were no risk. That was where he had first seen Pari. Once he'd heard Dory talking about him, he knew it was just a matter of time till they met. When Dory had told him she'd heard Pari was back from India and she wanted to see him, Spike had insisted on coming along. He still regretted that night—not that he'd stayed with Pari, no—but for the split it had caused with Dory. He felt guilty about that—and even more about the meth he'd sold her. No doubt it was fun to do, but the price was way too high. *Cheap in the short but expensive in the long,* he thought. *That drug robbed people of their souls—it took Dory's.* He knew now he shared responsibility for the way things went for both girls. He was their connection to the Super and to their drug use. He hadn't thought of himself as a pusher then, just a friend who wanted to share a good time...so he had thought.

He still hadn't gotten over the day Mary died. They'd just started to party and were driving out into the desert when a cop pulled them over. Dory panicked about the little baggie of meth she had. She'd bought meth from him whenever she couldn't afford anything else. Mary, always the cool one, grabbed it and swallowed the bag. It must have been partially open. An hour later, at St. Mary's

Hospital, she was dead. Dory was never the same after that. Now she was dead too, and it was his fault. He knew they'd taken Pari in to jail and that was also bad. He really liked the guy but, as usual, he'd fucked it up. He wished he'd never gotten involved with the Super. That guy got me in over my head, he thought. Spike was beginning to understand just how much he really needed to get out from under that grip.

☼

The Supervisor, George Oldfather, was beginning to feel the first touch of urgency, realizing that he had to shut down his operation before it was too late. He'd been a bit too careless and had to backtrack now very quickly to keep from being caught. The good thing was he had something on almost everyone, with a couple of glaring exceptions. Also, few people, if anyone, would suspect that the whole drug scenario was a blind to keep the focus off his real transgressions. *The way to keep that quiet is to misdirect at the right moment*, he assured himself. He couldn't do that if the focus came too early or from the wrong direction.

George looked over the elaborate emailed dinner invitation that had just popped into his inbox from Deels. He thought he probably had no choice but to attend. The phone rang while he was responding. He took a call and listened with annoyance. Supervisor Oldfather was beginning to sweat, and it wasn't Tucson's fabled heat. It was the sticky scrutiny of the public, through Zane and his inane radio program. He wasn't ready for that. *Damn Deels*, he thought, knowing where Zane's tip must have originated. He'd have to move a little faster, but that was okay. He liked speed.

☼

Cory always woke early, but today he was up at 4:00. He had a dinner party to plan. *Officer Moreno played his card correctly,* he thought. Cory rarely turned down the opportunity for a soirée. He had worked through the guest list for the first time yesterday and had come up with six and emailed them his formal, electronic dinner invitation. He had a series of them specially designed by his tech guy, Johnny.

Pari, Evy, Philip Moreno, Woody Madrone, Supervisor Oldfather and Carole Anne. He wasn't wild about inviting his ex, but he knew she was involved. Woody wouldn't like it either, but then Woody wasn't making up the guest list. He counted again and realized he was one short for the table, but a couple short for the right mix. *Oh yes, Pari's friend...Mr. Spike Smith. Amusing name, enigmatic fellow Also, perhaps Pari's clients.* Still, the list lacked a name, he knew, and the party a theme. The phone rang, Evy.

"Boss, I need to talk to you about George Oldfather."

"And?"

"You heard that weasel Zane on the radio?"

"No, but I am the one who put him on the trail." Evelyn did not respond. "Evy, I knew he would sniff out any impropriety and broadcast it. In any case, I gave him the tip about Oldfather's recent spending,"

"How did you know?"

"Because I know his loan officers."

Page 82

More silence from Evy.

"I can hear you fussing. They didn't reveal any confidential information. They assumed I was calling for a pre-approval. I knew Zane would chase out any rabbits, but I also knew you would easily discover from which hole they sprang."

He knew she would feel better about it now, but again he had her off balance. She launched into the rest of what she knew. "I found out a bit about where the money might be coming from. As you know, the supervisor has his fingers in the County Sheriff's department. The rumor is that seized drugs were being switched with bales of lookalikes before being burned. However, I don't see how that might fit into this murder."

"She was a drug user, Evy. She could have known something."

"That is true, but there may be other connections. It appears to me that Woody Madrone, and the Samaniego sisters, among others, were straw buyers for some entity on a few major land deals."

"Woody often bought land for possible subdivisions, but the Samaniego girls are a puzzle. Why do you find this suspicious?"

"These deals were with municipal properties and done prior to County announcements of land sales and trades."

"Fraud. Still, who is the mastermind and profiteer? I am sure the answer seems obvious."

"I've not found a direct link to Oldfather."

"Not surprising. He wouldn't leave obvious tracks. Who notarized and recorded the Deeds at County?"

"Dolores Samaniego." He paused for a moment before speaking.

"I see." He now knew the missing dinner guest and the theme for his gathering. "Evy, I will need to you make a few calls for a dinner party. I am sending emails but I want personal invitations on the phone from you as well."

"All right."

"Dolores Samaniego is not on this list, but you will call her after we are done, and suggest that she call me. Tell her I want to hold a wake for her daughters here."

"A wake?"

"Yes, my dear. Death _is_ serious business. The living need to celebrate the dead to live life fully." Cory knew Evy well enough to guess she was uncomfortable with the subject so he went on. "Death cannot be ignored by the living without peril. I'm emailing you the list now. On another subject, what did you find out about the chain of title on the house?"

"There is nothing recorded past your sale."

"Good, that is what I needed to know."

"Cory, I saw the original contract. I think you could have some issues."

He glared at the phone. "At this point, Evy, I want you to focus on Oldfather and Madrone. Any further inquiry into my dealings is off target." His sudden anger at her surprised him.

Evelyn agreed to the condition but Cory knew that would not be the end of it. One of the things he valued in her was her loyalty to the brokerage and to him, and that loyalty sometimes led her to go too far.

"When are you going to disclose your involvement? I would think it would be material to the sale."

Cory nearly lost it, but chose instead to hang up. *Sometimes,* he thought, *it is better to say nothing.*

Chapter 13: The Recorder

Dolores Samaniego listened to Evelyn Valdez's message while she took the morning paper and her coffee to the kitchen table. It was a built-in affair, made by her husband 30 years ago, just after they bought the house. They were newlyweds, and he'd wanted to recreate the diner booth where he'd proposed to her. When she and Carole Anne used to hang out, this was where they would gossip. Her daughter and Dorothea ate breakfast every day at this table growing up. The Formica was worn but still in good shape and clean. Dolores kept everything very clean. All these years later, even after so much sorrow, desperation and death, just sitting down in the booth still made her smile for a moment. A little smile, just for a moment—less every day.

Dolores couldn't decide exactly when life had started to sour, but she had a very good idea. It was clear to her now that things were not going to turn around. She also thought a reckoning might be due shortly, could not be long avoided. What she couldn't understand was why she just didn't come clean. *Why not?* She thought, *I have no one left to protect. I haven't since Mary died, really.* Once Mary had died, Dorothea completely pulled away and Dolores's husband Hernan also withdrew from her. Dolores thought it strange, but he seemed to show even more affection for Dorothea after Mary's death. For some reason she couldn't fathom, that hurt her too. Dolores couldn't understand her own reactions lately and that made her very angry. She and her husband ended up living in their house as if each was alone, hardly speaking until he died.

Her heart had already hardened to him by then and when he died she was almost glad. That made her feel even guiltier, and angrier because of the guilt. Yet with Dorothea, she felt nothing. Sometimes she thought perhaps she *should* feel guilty for not feeling anything, anything at all about the girl—but she couldn't, she wouldn't. She had decided Dorothea was a bad seed. Dolores was sure Dory was the one responsible for Mary's death, and for bringing that lech into their lives. She hoped eventually George Oldfather would take the blame for Dory. *A certain kind of justice*, she thought.

Dolores felt Dorothea was also responsible for the loss of her husband's love and ultimately for his death. *What else could I do but kick her out after that? What could anyone expect me to do, support her addictions?* The thought made her furious again. Almost as mad as she had been the last time she had seen Dory. It was good no one else had known about that. *Tough love*, she thought, *too bad it didn't work, but when it didn't work, Dorothea got what she deserved.* This was a refrain Dolores had repeated many times in the last week. Still, she knew she could put on a good show of grief. When Officer Moreno came to give her the news, she had managed to squeeze out a tear, and to look bewildered and lost. She had studied how people behaved when they were in grief, and she could do a good pantomime.

She also wondered why no one had come for her. *Perhaps this was it, perhaps the piper came as Cory Deels and one of his famous dinners.* She sighed, thinking she had no energy or time for a social gathering, let alone a wake...how could she pull herself together for that? Dolores found it harder every day to get up, to find a reason to make coffee, gather the paper, do the crossword, sit at this table. Still, she did it. Life had become a habit. A lonely, painful and bitter habit.

The message from Evelyn Valdez had been left yesterday, but she hadn't bothered to listen to it till now. Unfortunately, it seemed she had to respond. She stood up and walked to the tape recorder, pressing the button to rewind it. Mary and Dorothea had teased her about the machine, saying it must be as old as they were, it was. *No*

... now it was older than they will ever be. Still, it worked. She hit the "play" button:

"Hi Dolores, this is Evelyn Valdez, Cory Deels' office assistant. You might remember me—we've met a couple of times. Cory asked me to give you a call. First, he apologizes for the late request and offer, but he would like to know if you would be so kind as to call him to plan a dinner. He is offering to host a wake for your girls at his house. He said to mention that he remembers your playing Go with him fondly and is sorry that so much time has passed since you last played a game with him. He said the best condolence he can give you for all the death in your family is this gathering. We are all still adjusting to the shock of Dory's death, but perhaps this is a way to celebrate her life and Mary's.

Oh, and he asked me to mention that he wants to reconnect with his ex and hoped you might help with that, since you're friends. Carole Anne will be at the dinner, and he thought this might be good for everyone involved. Let me know...289-3335."

Not knowing what she was doing, Dolores violently swept the machine off the table. When it hit the ground, the tape began to reverse. Evelyn's words came out backwards and sounded evil, frightening. She flew into a rage and stomped on the machine. She brought her shoe down on the recorder, over and over until every last resemblance to an answering machine was gone.

She sat down again and wept, still shaking with her rage and the unexpected burst of anger. There was so much wrong with that message, with that invitation, with her life. She got up and walked to the broom closet in the hall and retrieved the dust pan and her broom. *What do I need a message machine for?* She thought. *If people want me, they can write, or come by.*

Yet as she was sweeping, she realized that the voice in the message had spoken the first human words she had heard in this house since Dorothea had left. So much silence. Dolores had stopped listening to the radio and the TV once Mary had died. That was how she had heard about Mary's death, on the late night news. Of course they didn't release her name, but the camera got a good picture of Dory and her friend Spike under the headline <u>Local Teen Dies of Drug Overdose</u>.

She sat back down and sipped her cold coffee, thinking about what to do. She knew Cory well enough to suppose he was aware of much more than he was letting on. She also figured that he had used the bit about Carole Anne as a little misdirection. Very like their Go games. He certainly must have known Dolores and Carole Anne were not speaking, and he knew she would know he knew that too.   She smiled, a hard, brittle smile. He had something to trade. He needed her, but was willing to give up something. Dolores knew his style of play very well, and now felt as though she just might have an edge. This message from him told her there was something in this for her. Perhaps she could use this generosity to her advantage. *He will know I am playing for an advantage, that is true, but he doesn't know everything,* she thought.

She'd made her decision. Dolores took the yellow slimline phone off the kitchen wall, careful to make sure the coils did not entwine. She admired it for a moment. It was as new looking and spotless as the day her husband gave it to her. She cleaned it after every use with the Lysol spray she kept on the kitchen counter—original scent of course.

She dialed the Deels house as she walked through the kitchen door to the screened in porch. The morning sun had not come over the roof into her yard and it was still chilly. Still she stepped out the screen door to the stoop as far as the phone would go. Old habit. She saw with displeasure that her bougainvillea had been nipped by last night's freeze. As the phone rang, a stray cat meowed and began to climb the steps. She grimaced and hissed at it, raising her foot. The cat fled. She realized someone had picked up while she had been hissing.

"Uh, Hello?" It was Evelyn.

"Hello Evelyn, this is Dolores Samaniego. Sorry, that was a cat."

"Hi Dolores, a cat. Just a moment, I'm driving, I'll pull over."

Dolores could hear amusement in Evelyn's voice. The knowledge that she'd been caught in this tiny lie re-awoke her anger, she considered hanging up but stopped herself. "Should I call you at another time?"

"No, no, my apologies. Okay, I'm ready."

"Please tell Cory I would be delighted to help in any way I can, and that I am grateful he has decided to honor my daughters in this way. When?"

"On the 4th, at 8:00"

"So soon? So late at night?"

"Sorry we are so late with the invitation, but apparently that is the best night for most of the guests. A few of them will not be able to arrive until that hour, so Cory decided the best thing was to have a late dinner party."

"Thank you, I'll be there. Please also tell him I would love to play a game with him sometime—if he has finally learned about ladders....I will call him personally, tomorrow. Please convey my words exactly."

"Certainly, I've noted what you said. I will let him know."

Dolores could tell by the chill in Evelyn's voice she thought this odd. So she reiterated, "Tell him Exactly."

"For certain. By the way, Dolores, I just wanted to say how sorry I am this has happened, My brother died a year ago so I know how you feel."

Dolores was stunned. If Evelyn had been standing in front of her at that moment she would have slapped her. *Bitch*, she thought, *you have no clue how I feel...shut the fuck up*.

Still, she smiled as she spoke the ritual words back. "Thank you so much, I appreciate your concern." Still, she couldn't quite keep the frost out of her tone, and Evelyn seemed to have sensed her anger, muttering a quick "Bye" before hanging up the phone.

Dolores went back in and pulled out the paper, puzzle section, and sat back down in the booth. Picking up her pen, she whipped out the Ken Ken and the Sudoku in record time. She was ready to spar.

Chapter 14: All Souls Procession

Carole Anne Michaels had more reason than most to join the All Souls Procession, though this was the first year she would march. In former years she had taken out-of-town friends to the event and had even been paid by a group of Japanese tourists to act as a guide and interpret it, with the help of Dolores Samaniego. This year though, she was a participant. This had been a season of death for her. She desperately needed to grieve, to find a way through her angry, bitter mood. In the past she had wondered at the real motive behind the amazing costumes and elaborately painted faces. She no longer wondered.

Now she peered into her pocket mirror, examining the crude skull-paint that obliterated her features. It was a startling transformation. An hour ago her tough but classic beauty might have turned heads, but the ghoul in the glass would drive the desperate away. She grinned broadly and laughed at the death rictus that stared back.

Prominent cheekbones make a good skull, she thought. Next, she fixed the drywall stilts to her legs and dropped the black robe down over them. She stood up and pulled the huge paper mâché head off the top of the bookcase. It was handy to have those two extra feet the stilts provided. She couldn't decide which face should look forward and which back...her father or her daughter. In the end she decided to add her own painted death mask, placing her father in front with her daughter looking behind, it seemed appropriate. She wore her own skull hidden inside the two, and that seemed appropriate too. Placing the mask on her shoulders, she began to walk the few blocks from her home on 3rd Avenue to the beginning of the gathering.

As she walked, she remembered the spiel she used to parrot to the tourists. At the time, the words meant little to her, but today they took on meaning and significance. She supposed it was because she had finally experienced real loss. She spoke them out loud as she walked, and the costume freed her to speak them with drama and flair. Random people she passed clapped and laughed as she passed them, and began to walk along so they could hear the whole piece

"The Tucson All Souls Procession is one of the most iconic regional festivals in the US. Every year, hundreds of artists and many thousands of local citizens assemble in dark costume a few days after Halloween. I invite you to join us! We march together in remembrance of the dead. We walk to celebrate the fleeting quality of life. Our procession winds its way through downtown and ends in a powerful convocation where we burn our letters to the dead in a pyre. Our procession is rooted in our local traditions, created by a grieving artist, and recreated each year by all of us. It is a bizarre and joyous event and it may be hard for you to grasp, but try; you will be rewarded. Do not expect a party or lark—this is not Mardi Gras. Our solemn celebration defies easy understanding, but I warn you, it is addictive. Remember, the pictures you see held by the marchers are of their dear and newly dead. Respect them! Each costume and mask is an echo of a lost love, a child too early to the grave, or a dear friend's untimely passage through that dark and unknown door. You will also journey though that passage. But join me before you do! The fire, the drums and the dancing skeletons will help you celebrate the transitory nature of life."

Many people were now following her. She had become the leader of a parade to the procession and had ceased to be herself. Instead, she was the enigmatic archetype of death embodied in her mask. Carole Anne clenched the paper in her sleeve pocket as she strode down the street while her spirit grew to fill her puppet. *I am striding, she thought, moving swiftly through the droll battlefield of life.* She picked up her speed and soon outpaced the crowd. It was exhilarating to fly at such a speed over the heads of others. She felt like a lioness threading her way through a herd of wildebeest with precision and awesome speed. She felt all-powerful and capable of anything in her anonymity. Then she caught the foot of a stilt in a pavement crack and nearly fell. All that exhilaration turned in an instant to fear and embarrassment.

She found a low wall and sat, as if on a high bench, to catch her wits. The crowd parted and went on their way to the gathering place. Remembering the paper, she pulled it out and recited the communication she'd inscribed. "O daughter, O father, forgive me for all I meant to do and did not, for all I meant to say and did not. I am sorry I cut you from my life. Now, my only gift is tears, yet I cannot give even those. You needed me but I was absent, and I apologize. You loved me but I rejected you, and I apologize. You asked of me only what I should have given freely to anyone ... but I withheld my love, my comfort and my all from you. I am sorry."

The words took on the cadence of a prayer to her ears. She knew there was a powerful truth in what she had written, but the feelings eluded her and slipped through her heart as wind through an empty city. She waited, hoping to feel the swell of tears, but her eyes remained dry. She did not know why her heart refused to open. These words, her words, rang empty and hollow. *I am stone,* she thought. *It is too late.* She sighed and set out again, loping now with more caution and reserve, hoping that once she placed the message in the vessel and watched it burn she might be able to release this terrible burden and grieve.

The revelers were finding their places and she rejoined the raucous throng. She mixed into the herd unknown to all. Some of the participants knew each other but many desired anonymity. *We are like Arabic women in chador, behind the veil.* The idea was almost erotic to her. The sun had set behind the Tucson Mountains, and now the Catalinas began to glow a brilliant vermillion. Color suffused the faces of those few who had not donned their paint and it soaked the assembly in a bloody hue.

She wandered through the giant puppets and macabre mannequins at the beginning of the procession and watched them rehearse a pantomimed dance. Tourists and onlookers strolled through the crowd taking pictures and laughing, occasionally asking for a picture or blessing. She was stopped several times by people admiring her costume. At one point a geisha, who had been following a man dressed as the Buddha, stopped and looked at her, bowing in respect. Carole Anne bowed in return. The Buddha spoke, "Carole Anne, I'm not surprised to see you here."

"Cory! How the hell did you know it was me?" She said, but he ignored her and wandered off into the crowd. *God, he can be annoying*, she thought, *He can't get off his high horse even dressed as the Buddha.* Seeing this player out of her past was disconcerting and upsetting, but she shoved all those feelings down and put that part of her life out of her mind. *I'm here for a new start, not a dive into past messes.* It wasn't hard to be distracted in the procession though.

A drumming corp began beating an Afro-Cuban cadence. Other drummers began competing rhythms, fifes and flutes, bells and whistles filled the air. Someone was singing, chanting in an unknown tongue and she hummed along. All this was answered by an amazing cacophony of Gamelon bells played by people dressed as Hanuman and his monkey troop. Shadow puppets, Aztec dancers and fire-breathers swirled around her followed by Goths, Mariaches, and Celtic gods.

Carole Anne slipped through the group and made her way to the cauldron. She saw it was a thing of beauty, metal, yet cut in filigree design. She would later throw her prayer into this vessel. She shivered from the first chill of coming winter, but the crowd was heated and the scent of bodies, close and hot, filled her nostrils. She smelled patchouli and sweat, gardenias and the thick odor of herb—a joint was being passed and she could tell the weed was powerful. Her nostrils flared as she smelled something very familiar, a bitter spice, but she could not place it...frankincense or myrrh? She wandered through the crowd looking for the source, enjoying the stilts and the feeling of being taller than almost everyone. As the dark fell and the group coalesced, Carole Anne took her place behind a group of Buddhist monks, led by the geisha and Buddha. They were chanting and repeating "Om mani padme hum..." The words entered her heart, lightened her mood and soon her feet were moving to the drummers up ahead.

She walked with them a mile, then two, and now many people began to dance with the drums. Again, Carole Anne caught the scent of something, someone familiar...*who or what is it?* She wondered. She looked carefully through the crowd around her. On her left, a man wearing a horse-head pranced next to an Aztec Priest. In front of her a group of ten mask-wearers danced in slow motion, each with a picture of their dead dance instructor painted on their backs. Behind her, a dozen people worked an elaborate mechanism that moved the bones of a fluorescent dinosaur. To her right a hunchbacked manikin cavorted, leered at her. The minimus was chained around the neck and clothed in fur. He was not the source of the scent: he smelled of animals, mildew and the odor of a man who has not bathed in many years. The holder of the chain, though, was a question. He was a two-faced man who wore a bleeding Christ over his face and a Nixon mask to cover the back of his head. He'd dressed in red robes, with a knotted rope for a belt.

Carole Anne had seen him several times now in the crowd. First, as everyone gathered, he'd posed lewdly before tourists taking pictures. Later, he had bumped into her as she had joined the monks, and then had wandered off with the bagpipe troupe. Now here he was again and she got the feeling he was watching her, even as he led the dwarf off to the other side of the street. He pulled cruelly, but the manikin seemed to enjoy the strangle.

They were approaching the end. Ahead, an ornamental bier stood waiting for the vessel. *A thousand ghouls circle the pyre, ten thousand more are on their way,* she thought. Carole Anne took her long strides through the crowd and as the vessel was placed on the bier, she said again the prayer and tossed the paper on the heap. She repeated the message of that prayer like a holy mantra;

"O daughter, O father, forgive me for all I meant to do and did not, for all I meant to say and did not. I am sorry I cut you from my life. Now, my only gift is tears, yet I cannot give even those. You needed me but I was absent, and I apologize. You loved me but I rejected you, and I apologize. You asked of me only what I should have given freely to anyone ... but I withheld my love, my comfort and my all from you. I am sorry."

Her feelings began to swell. Drums joined, dancers pitched and wove around her and a frenzy erupted as the Aztec lit the pyre. *Let it go*, she thought, *let them both go with the smoke.* The fire leapt and the tension in her chest broke. She felt stinging water well up her eyes, *At last,* she thought. Then the odor returned and with it the two-faced man, who grabbed her hand and almost pulled her over. The noise of the crowd was deafening, but he shouted and a few words got through the noise and their masks.

"Come with me, puta. You and I will end this story tonight, one way or another."

She could not place the voice but felt a cold jab in her lower back.

The scent recalled a memory and then she knew who he was. The Buddha stood right behind the two faced man as if he was the director of some sinister play. *Why would Cory Deels be here with that low-life?* She thought. Suddenly, a shock went through her and she knew who had killed her little girl. She tried to run, but the pull of Two-Face's hand broke her balance and she began to twist on the stilts. The Aztec, a mariachi and the geisha had also been watching this scene and now they joined the fray. The Aztec's mask slipped for a moment and she realized with a shock who he was. *There's too much going on!* She panicked, realizing she might be the next victim in a murder spree.

Carole Anne stuck out a foot in a wild attempt to regain her poise. She kicked two-face savagely in the gut and then her foot slammed into the geisha and hit something hard. A gun went off and she felt the bullet pierce the mask above her head. Then she was free, running on the stilts, careening back and forth, dodging the now terrified participants. Despite her horror she almost laughed. It was great to be alive. What she was witnessing was priceless. It looked like a scene from a bad zombie movie: the All Souls procession had become a panicked mob of the undead.

Chapter 15: A Life Estate

The day after Halloween Pari gave his updated journal to Cory. The day after that, they met in his office to discuss the way forward. Pari had not been inside Cory's office before this meeting. He expected to see more of the rich overstatement he'd seen in the rest of the house but in contrast to his quarters, Cory's office was a statement in modern severity. Hard edges, clean lines, Eams chairs for clients, and a neutral color palate said this was a place for serious work. The only concession to decoration Pari could see was the collection of gorgeous photos of local homes hung on the walls. Each was a multimillion dollar property in one of the main Tucson styles: Modern Adobe fusion, Territorial, Santa Fe, Spanish and Modern Industrial. He noticed that on the wall behind Cory, and slightly above his desk was a flat screen for displaying documents and photos to his clients. Pari assumed the desk which was totally uncluttered, functioned as monitor, keyboard and filing cabinet.

Cory looked up for a moment as Pari entered and motioned for him to sit on one of the chairs clustered around a large glass table. With a swipe of his hand Cory switched on the table. Before Pari was his scanned journal, sections highlighted and underlined. He felt overwhelmed, as if he were back in school, waiting for the results of a test. Pari could see that this level of tech might seriously win over the higher end customers, and perhaps give Cory the advantage in a negotiation. He was glad Cory was on his side. At last Cory looked up from his desk and directed his attention at Pari. God. *What am I in for?* He thought. However, Cory's words were not what Pari expected.

"Young man, I owe you an apology."

Pari was at a loss, "What? I don't know what you mean."

"I am sure you don't. That too is my fault. When I hired you, no, let's start earlier—when I persuaded you to come and join my profession, I owed you a duty to guide and train you. I have not fulfilled my duty. Instead, I tossed you into the waters and expected you to swim."

Pari was unsure how to respond, "Cory, none of this is your fault."

"That is true, but sins of omission are still sins. I also want to thank you, as you have made me take a deeper look at the way I have been doing business. Up to this point I have always hired agents who were already successful and have their systems down and tested. You are my first new agent, but I have learned from you. The candor of your journal calls me to step up my game, and so I shall. But I want to ask you a favor."

Pari was embarrassed by the unexpected praise. He had expected a dressing down, not an apology, and he was eager to please and help in anyway he could. "Anything, what can I do for you?"

"I need you to help me draw up a policy manual and a set of standards. I have had one, of course, but too loosely defined and full of jargon. It would be unintelligible to a new agent."

"I don't think I'm in a position to give you advice, I really don't know much of anything."

"That is precisely why you will be such a big help. I know what should be done and the ways to do the needful, but I need your help communicating those ideas to someone who knows very little about Real Estate."

Pari quickly agreed to the job, excited about helping Cory refine his business. Also, he knew from his medical experience that the best way to learn something was to review it for others. However, as happy as he was about the future, the present situation still weighed on him and he was hoping Cory had some sort of plan to flush out Dory's killer and clear him of the charges. When he brought this point up, Cory seemed much less concerned than he would have supposed. However, once he spent some time talking about the potential problems with the title of the house, a deed he knew about and how he planned to sort things out, Pari felt some relief.

"Also, Pari, I have decided to host a wake for the young lady and her sister."

"Wow. That's nice, but why?"

Cory closed the screens with a gesture and sat back. "I am not being 'nice,' This dinner party has several purposes, and not all of them involve Dory's death. As for you, I am quite sure if I can get the right people in one room, you will be cleared. Also, since Woody is not represented, we want him and Carole Anne Michaels present with your clients to clear up any issues around what might be an extant Estate for Life."

"What is an Estate for Life"

"It means someone has been given the right to Quiet Enjoyment of the property, but without any other rights apart from the right to convey the right. In other words, it is like an indefinite lease, until you die, without the need to pay rent to anyone. Also, you can sell it or give it to another....it goes with the land so if your people buy the property and the Deed is invoked they may not be able to live in the property.

"Good God!" Pari said.

"Right now, though, I would like to be sure that anyone who might be trying to dupe the public about other matters comes to justice."

Pari found this conversation enticing and wanted to follow up, but just then Evy stepped into the office to hand Cory some documents. She also let Pari know his clients had arrived.

"Where are they?" he asked.

"I've put them into the conference room across from my desk," she said.

Pari looked to Cory for direction, but he just waved both of them off, apparently already absorbed by the contracts Evy had brought him.

As they walked the short hall to the front of the brokerage, Pari saw Evy look him over in a calculating way. It made him quite uncomfortable, and he was aware he was showing his nervousness. Evy made him a bit uncomfortable; he thought it must be her overt sexuality.

"So, I hear through the grapevine you can be quite the ladies' man. I always assumed you were gay."

Pari was shocked. "Which grape got squeezed and gave you that juice?" he said, trying to appear cooler than he was.

"I've got contacts, but don't worry, I won't bite you—even though you might be tasty." She laughed and he blushed.

He knew now where this news must have come from. *So much for police confidentiality,* he thought. "Don't believe everything you hear Evy. If I did, I might have done some of my own cross-examination at the police station."

"Touché Pari!"

Pari knew he'd gained some points with her and felt good about it. His clients were thumbing though some listing magazines when he arrived. He'd told them on the phone there were a few problems with the purchase that could be material to the sale. At this point they were nervous about what might come next. He thought most people would have run from the house once they realized a theft had taken place. Happily, Dana and Rupert Brooks told him that could have happened anywhere. Later, after the murder in the atrium, Pari absolutely expected them to flee, but when they didn't he decided that as emergency room interns—and now doctors—they saw death every day and had no superstitions. As Rupert had told him, "I suspect nearly every spot on earth has been the location of a death at one point, so why would we worry about this one?"

Even the fact that Pari had been arrested as a suspect did not dissuade them. He thought they assumed he was innocent because they were friends. *Of course,* Pari thought, *they also know the house is unique and exactly what they want.* When he questioned them it turned out their main concern was whether the glass in the atrium had been repaired. *Go figure.*

Before he had a chance to discuss the problems that had arisen, Dana suggested they visit the house one more time. Pari thought that was an excellent plan; they could then have a conversation about next steps on the way. He figured that would allow his clients to digest the information he was about to give them before revisiting the house. Their inspection period was expiring at the end of the following day, the day of Cory's dinner party, so they needed to wrap up their investigations.

Pari took Anklam Road past St. Mary's Hospital where Rupert would be working. He thought they should take the drive over Gates Pass to see how much time that commute would use. He knew Dana would be working at Northwest Medical center, so he thought the road out Picture Rocks would be better for her commute, and they would take that route on the way back. No one minded the ride; Pari always found it spectacular, winding up through ironwood forests, past massive saguaros and up to a knife edge view of both the Tucson Valley and the Altar Valley to the Southwest. When they came down that west side, he pointed out clusters of Teddy Bear Cholla glowing gold in the sun. He knew they looked almost soft enough to touch. "Beware," he said, "sometimes the most inviting and beautiful things snare you in an intractable grip. So I have learned."

He drove them past Old Tucson, the fake frontier town used as a movie set, and then north through the Saguaro National Monument while he covered his points, beginning with an apology. "Guys I'm sorry that what I am about to tell you missed my attention until now. My excuse is that I'm new, but still, I should have done the research."

"Okay" Rupert looked wary, "How bad is it, Pari?"

"Well, bad enough. The first thing is that it turns out my boss used to own this house. In fact, he built it."

"How is that a bad thing?" Dana asked. "Judging from your boss's house and business I would guess he built it well and took care of it. But Pari, I thought you said Mr. Madrone built the house."

"Well, he did, they both did, but that is not bad, just to clarify. They were business partners and Cory had Woodrow Madrone build the house for him. I would agree that this is a good thing, as my boss is fastidious. Also, I understand Madrone is one of the city's best builders. Last, my broker is providing you with an additional disclosure statement which explains in great detail everything he knows about the house."

"Why didn't he tell us, or tell you all this earlier?" Rupert asked.

"That is my fault alone. I didn't submit my sale file right away, so Mr. Deels did not find out which house it was until after I was arrested. Also, because I had not submitted the file, he had no way to contact you until we spoke. Again, I apologize. If this is too much information to process let me know."

Dana sounded decisive to Pari: "No, none of this matters to me, this house is perfect. Is that all?"

"I wish it were." *Here comes the hard part*, he thought. "The next item is something I learned just this morning and I'll try to get it right. It turns out, if you buy this property you may not have the right to live in it." Pari could see Rupert stiffen with this news.

"How's that?" he said, "How can that be? If we own it, we own it, right?"

"Well, not exactly. When you buy a property you are buying a big bundle of rights, but almost never all of them. It could be the right to occupy the house is not for sale at this particular moment."

"Explain please. This is a new idea for me." Pari loved Dana's inflections; they came from her Norweigan parents.

Just then Pari swerved a bit as two coyotes ran across the road in front of them. For a moment they were diverted by the animals as well as the magnificence of the natural world around them. Above him, Pari saw a hawk soar in an updraft, while below, a cactus wren poked her head from a saguaro. On the ground, Gambel Quail ran to a creosote bush. *All that life in one glimpse!* Pari wondered then how any man could own such beauty. The idea of ownership seemed foreign to him. He knew the world had been here for eons before him, and that it would exist far longer after he was gone.

The words of his favorite teacher at the U of A, an ecologist who left teaching to join a radical green movement now made more sense to him. "How can a man, whose life is but a moment, plunder this treasure?" his professor had said. "The span of our lives can be lost in the blink of God's eye—so how can ephemeral beings, such as we, own the permanent? Surely the earth belongs to all its creatures. Men should only be allowed to steward this paradise, not pick its flesh until the dry bones lie lifeless, white and barren."

Pari wondered then at the underpinnings of his new profession. He looked across the valley to an old open pit mine whose sterile tailings still leached toxic metals into the arroyo below. He tried to focus on the issue at hand. *The world is complicated! I know simple answers are a trap, but they can be seductive.* Pari knew his job was not to settle the grand questions of human society but to explain the rules of ownership as they exist and to protect his client's interests and rights. *At least I'm selling this property to people who I know will take care of it.* He launched into an explanation, wondering how this news would go down.

"Ownership of property amounts to the granting of certain rights pertaining to a piece of land and what is on it. Usually you do not own all the rights. This idea stems from the granting of deeds to titled gentry by the King in ancient times. That is where we get the words, title and deed. These rights may include water and mineral rights; the right to quiet enjoyment; the right to determine who may have access to your property to use it for hunting, fishing, planting, or the right to pass though it; and the right to occupy the property itself. There are other rights but the important point here is that each of these rights can be owned separately from the others, or may be deeded—given or sold for periods of time."

Dana piped up again. "So, you are saying it is possible to buy the property but not be able to enjoy it? This is such an odd idea."

"Think about your current living situation. You have bought the rights of occupancy and quiet enjoyment from your landlord with your lease. Your landlord owns the property, but he has given those rights to you for as long as your tenancy lasts. Even if he sells the property, your lease takes precedence since he cannot sell what he does not own. He can only sell the benefit he receives from it, your rent."

Pari saw that this seemed to satisfy Dana, but Rupert still looked doubtful.

"I'm getting a little concerned, are you saying this property is leased?"

"No, not leased. However there is a chance that a deed which was issued by my boss twenty years ago is still in effect. This would be a cloud on the title of the property we need to clear up. A cloud on the title means not everything is clear about the ownership of a right. The deed I am referring to is called an "Estate For Life." That deed grants the right to occupy the property for the duration of the life of the owner of the deed, but it does not convey all the other rights, like the right to sell the property. The person who owns the property now, Mr. Madrone, is not the person who has that deed. Also, this deed was not mentioned in the seller's disclosure statement. Perhaps that was an oversight, but it is also possible the person who owns or owned that deed has lost it, leased it, sold it or perhaps even offered the owner a quit claim."

"What is a quit claim?" Dana asked.

"That is a deed which relinquishes all rights to a property over to another entity."

"How is it that no one knows? Shouldn't such things be recorded?"

"Yes, that would be best, but even if it is not recorded, it is still valid if it can be produced."

"What does this mean to us?" Rupert again.

"It depends. If the owner of the deed has issued a quit claim, then it will not affect you. If the deed is outstanding then she or he would have the right to claim occupancy at any time as long as she or he is alive. I know this is confusing, but my boss and I have a plan to resolve the issue, to find the deed and remove it or else allow you to cancel the sale." Pari could see this did not sit well with Dana.

"Cancel! No. This is our house. We must find another way." With that Pari turned off the motor as they had arrived at the property.

"My boss is having a dinner in which all the parties who have an interest in this home or who have been involved in it and the events around it will attend. He thinks we can settle it then, tomorrow, with everyone at the same table." Pari could see they were both over the worst. "So, I take it you still want to buy the house?"

"Yes!" said Dana.

"If we can also buy the right to live in it!" Rupert was less enthusiastic, but Pari could hear the excitement in his voice.

"Okay, then I strongly suggest you attend the dinner party." They consulted for a moment and Dana spoke up.

"We would love to come. However, now I want to walk though my home one more time. Do you think the glass is repaired?"

"Oh, yes, and I sent the inspection report to the seller; he has already done the repairs suggested even without our asking. Let's take a good look at those." Pari already knew they would buy the house, no matter what.

Chapter 16: The Past Passes

Carole Anne parked her Harley on Convent and walked up the steps to the Deels house. She'd seen the kid, Pari, leave with a couple of clients, so she knew he wouldn't get in the way. She hoped Cory was home and receptive. The gates were locked, but, on cue, his voice greeted her.

"Hello, my dear, so nice to see you after all these years."

Dry sarcasm, I don't need it! "Cut it, Cory. Let me in so we can talk face to face."

"Why should I? You are already invited for dinner tomorrow night, isn't that enough? Besides, I am in the midst of preparations."

"That's exactly why I'm here—your dinner. I have some news to tell you that might help the purpose of your dinner, or perhaps not...your choice. That, and I need some professional advice. I'm counting on a little lingering respect, if not love, for the mother of your son. Can you manage it?"

The gate opened to the passadizo and shortly thereafter so did the one to the central courtyard. She'd always found this entrance pretentious and creepy, but she guessed it worked for his purposes. Cory announced that she could find him in the kitchen, so, Carole Anne walked through the inner gardens on the way to the main kitchen, marveling at the different paths their lives had taken. Cory loved the finer things in life, and he gathered them around him, but Carole Anne did not.

I love the funner things in life: freedom, riding my bike, traveling, she thought. Her wild spirit did not tame itself to a householder lifestyle. *Sometimes that gets me into trouble, but its worth it.* She knew the risks, but on the whole, she liked her life. *Ultimately, that was really what broke our marriage,* she thought; *he's a householder and I'm a gypsy.* She was old enough to know that the affairs she'd had were just her way of breaking bonds she could not bear to wear. Still, though she'd had very little good to say about him over the years, she was grateful for what he had done for her and for her son. *A pity I didn't have the same luck with my daughter,* she thought, instantly ashamed at her callousness.

She stopped at the fountain, breathing in the delicious scent. The Mexican lime was in its second bloom. The smell of citrus recalled her childhood in California, but now that sweetness soured. She remembered her mom telling her how she had met Carole Anne's dad at Altamont. It was one of her mother's favorite stories. "Danny Angelo was what they called your dad, he was an angel and a devil, but I loved him at first sight." Years had not quieted the voice in her head...her mother's voice. She supposed it was because her mom had died when she was still a kid. For Carole Anne, Mom would always be in her late 20s.

A delivery truck drove by and belched out a cloud of acrid fumes that drifted through the breezeway into the garden mixing with the scent of lime blossoms. That odor brought back more memories, and her mother's voice finished her story one more time. "He was one of the Hell's Angels you know. Mick hired them for security at the concert and well, you know, the boys in the band were fond of me, but I just clung to my Angelo after that." She knew her mom, Willow Michaels, was one of the Stones' groupies, but Carole Anne doubted she had really known the members of the band. There was, however, no doubt her dad had been a biker— she'd inherited her love of bikes from him. Her folks never married, but Carole Anne spent her childhood near an orange grove in Pasadena until after her mom had died. Carole Anne had lived there until her dad was arrested for breaking her arm one night while drunk and raging. After that she didn't want to remember anything about her life with Danny. *He did me wrong, but why am I still ashamed?* She knew that feeling was common with abused children, but knowing didn't help her.

Her dad had contacted her earlier this year, once he found out he had lung cancer. She refused to see him and he died within a week. She wished now she had met with him and forgiven him. That might have helped her. She wondered if her own kids felt as conflicted about her as she did about her folks. She could see she had become her father. *Sweet Jesus, don't things ever get better? This day sucks.*

All this introspection was making her feel worse, so Carole Anne made her way into the kitchen and found Cory at the Wolfe range. She saw he still made an unholy mess when he cooked—the island behind him was littered with spices, chopped onions, garlic, ginger and chilies. She watched him, waiting for a moment to break in. He was stirring a wok while mustard and caraway popped in hot oil, then he threw in a handful of onions, stirred in a tray heaped with piles of brightly colored spices, added ginger and garlic paste and the chiles. The pungent scents escaped the commercial exhaust and hit Carole Anne's nose with the force of a small bomb. Her eyes watered and she unexpectedly sneezed.

"Good Lord, cover your mouth!"

Never one for a polite hello, she thought. "Sorry, I didn't expect to be gassed when I walked in." After the initial assault the aroma was enticing. She could smell the lemon grass—he must be making a Thai sauce. "Satay?"

"No," he said, "but not too far off. This will be a chickpea thickened green coconut chili for marinating and coating skewered and grilled shrimp. Appetizer. I am finished with this, it must rest." He turned off the burner, removed his apron and tossed it into a little shoot for kitchen laundry. "Are you hungry?"

"No. Well, yes I am, actually."

"Come with me, I've got some leftover ratatouille and kofta in the fridge over in the games room."

She followed him over the arched bridge that spanned this part of the garden to the North side of the house and noticed the koi in the garden stream were now more than a foot long each. The elegant life, she thought, finding it both alluring and stifling. She remembered how much he loved to create the right atmosphere, to feed people and nurture them...those were what she thought of as his best traits. Rare in men, she thought. She felt deep regret for losing what she had never really had...*could I have had it? Cory can be a horse's ass, a complete know it all son-of-a-bitch; but he is also thoughtful and goes out of his way to help. Too bad I've never figured out how to accept help.*

The French doors into the game room were open to the courtyard, she looked the room over as they entered. This was where Cory let his hair down a bit. He'd play any game, but was fond of Bridge, and Go. *Games of strategy and cunning,* she thought. She saw that the Go board was set up and in the middle of a game. That board was where she had first met Dolores Samaniego, though on the base, where the Samaniegos then lived. When she and Cory first met, he was already friends with Dolores and her husband Hernan. Sometimes Dolores and Cory played games on this board. She remembered the first time she saw the two of them playing together. Dolores had just won, or established a path to victory, that seemed to be the sense of it to her—a path to victory was as good as a win. That was the only time you really saw emotion on Dolores's face, when she won a Go game. She was telling Cory about ladders and how to head them off. Carole Anne had liked it that Dolores was strong enough to gloat a bit in her victory. It was that trait that brought them together as friends. She examined the rest of the space.

This was the room was between Cory's and her son Raphael's bedrooms. She understood that now Pari Workingboxwalla was staying there. It galled her. She wished she knew exactly why Raphie had fled to India, but she thought her imaginings were probably about right. He shared a bit of her wild spirit. *At least he's in an ashram looking for truth instead of taking drugs till he dies.* She bit her lip for her continued oblique references to Dory—it was as though, despite her prayer at the All Soul's Procession, she couldn't stop blaming Dory for her own murder. She watched Cory pull a couple of plates out of the cupboard on the South Wall and dish up lunch from the fridge. They sat at the card table nearest the garden.

"Well Cass, what can I do for you?"

No one had ever called her that but Cory and Dolores, and not him for quite a while. Despite herself she teared. The words caught in her throat. She hated getting emotional. Still she spoke, "I've made a mess of things, Cory, and I have nowhere to turn but to you. I'm sorry."

With that she came unglued. She sobbed so violently she could not catch her breath. Cory held her, and to her it seemed as though the years melted away, and she was a young girl again needing support and love. *We've had common goals,* she thought. *I only have the people in my life, no others. I can't exchange them. If I embrace them, my life is full; if I reject them, I am an empty and bitter woman.* Her heart softened to him, after so many years. *It's good to be held.*

Cory spoke, "Where shall we begin? I already know you lost or gave away the deed I gave you."

"How?"

"Woody came by and told me he thought you no longer had it."

"So that's why he decided he could sell?"

"He always had the right to sell, but only you had the right to occupy. Why didn't you record the deed?"

"At first we were happy and married and it didn't seem to matter. Then, once we split up, Woody and I found an agreement. He paid me rent to stay in the house. That way I got to travel and do what I wished and he didn't have to buy me out. I always meant to get around to it, but it never really seemed important."

"And then?"

"I gave it to Dory."

"Dorothea Samaniego?"

"Yes, she was my daughter."

Cory coughed, and stirred the plate of food with his fork. *Well, that removed his hunger*, she thought. Carole Anne, however, had developed a sudden appetite. She imagined Cory was counting back. It wasn't hard, she knew he knew how old Dory had been when she died, a little less than one year younger than their son. Cory cleared his throat and got up for a beer. He kept his back to her while he opened and poured it into a chilled mug. He took a sip and sighed. She waited for him to speak.

"How? Carole Anne..."

"Cory, she wasn't yours..."

She tried to explain but looking at his face she saw old wounds had opened again. How could something so far in the past reawaken fresh as the day it happened?

They'd met 23 years ago at the Triple T Truck Stop. He'd just transferred to Davis Monthan AFB in Tucson from Ellsworth in Minot, North Dakota. She'd driven in that day from Barstow on her Harley. *It was a case of opposites attract,* she thought. *That, and the fact that Cory's parents had just died. He only went for me because he was raw from the loss, and the fact that he knew I had no other place to stay.* He'd told her he'd inherited money from his folks, and eventually they decided to build a house. That's how they'd met Woody. She'd heard from Dolores that he was *the* hot young builder in town. Carole Anne convinced Cory to work with him and Woody persuaded Cory to build his house on land the builder owned over in the Tucson Mountains. When the costs ran over the original bid, they went into partnership. By that time, they'd all become friends.

Cory and Carole Anne moved into the house before it was even completed, got pregnant and then married. Unfortunately, Woody and Carole Anne had the real chemistry, even if that chemistry was furtive and on the edge of violent. Whenever Woody walked near Carole Anne, her nostrils flared; she couldn't help but inhale his scent. He knew it and teased her unmercifully, always standing a little too close, brushing up against her with seeming randomness. Her nights with Cory were always more intense and violent after such an encounter. Nevertheless, Carole Anne did not consummate her passion with Woody, Cory was too important to her. *Life finally intervened*, she thought, *as Desert Storm. If Cory had not been posted to the war in Iraq right after Raphael was born, none of this would have happened.*

She assumed Cory was still piecing it together, "Yes, Cory, Woody was her father."

"So, this happened after I left for Iraq?"

"That was the first time for Woody and me. I got pregnant right away. I couldn't tell you then, I didn't even tell Woody. After I missed my period, I cut him out of my life. I told him I was too guilty to see him again and cut him off completely. He was such a lady's man, he just said okay and moved on to someone else. He didn't come back, and I didn't see him till after you returned. I stayed out in that lonely house and didn't see anyone but Dolores and Hernan Samaniego. She'd bring me food and necessities. Dolores and Hernan were the only people I told about my pregnancy. You know they had been trying to get pregnant for a long time and it just seemed natural. They wanted kids so badly they asked if they could take Dory before I even thought of it.

Then, right after we agreed, Dolores got pregnant. Dolores's mom was a midwife, so she was in on it too and we all agreed to keep the news from you, from everyone, even the girls. That worked until Mary and Dory were in their teens...then they found out. We had the girls in April, you came home at the end of May. You know the rest. Once you came home I just couldn't keep Woody out of my mind and...I'm sorry Cory, I just couldn't stay with you...too much guilt and regret."

"My God,"

She marveled that he had been so totally blind to such huge events.

"And you say Woody does not know either?"

"No. I thought he'd suspect when Dory moved in with him, and then I thought he'd know for sure once she showed him the deed. I think he was fond of her despite himself and he assumed she had stolen it and forged my name. So when he called me to ask, I just agreed with that. I'm not sure why, even now. Maybe I was afraid he'd ask too many questions and find out he was her father. Now I wish I had told him."

"But what possessed you to transfer the deed to Dory?"

"I told myself I gave it to her because she was in trouble and needed a place to stay. I see now the truth was that I was trying to make myself feel better, to cover my guilt for leaving her, trying to make it all better. At first I thought maybe meeting her and telling her a little about why I gave her up might help her quit using, but it blew up in my face. She was angry and we ended up fighting. Then she went back and confronted Dolores. Dolores and Dory got into it and Dolores kicked her out. I talked with Dolores to try to patch things up but it got even worse. In the end, I think I signed the deed over to Dory to win her love, and to give her a place to live...but it meant nothing to her."

This is how the past passes, she thought, *we understand each other and then forgive the old hurts.*

"What happened to the deed?"

She shook her head. "I don't know; Dory must have hidden it away."

"Cass, I think you should stay here until the dinner. Are you willing?"

She nodded. "I'm willing, but why?"

"Too much violence in the air and too many reasons why there might be more. Let's keep you safe." She followed him back through his quarters, to the secret guest room off the greenhouse. She knew he used it as his safe-house, though had never understood why a Realtor would need one. *Perhaps he's paranoid...or maybe he has secrets I know nothing about.* It went against her instincts to let him protect her, but she was feeling unsettled and needed a safe place to rest.

Chapter 17: Eagle's Nest

George Oldfather ran the Humvee up to the top of Swan Road as fast as he could push it, then made a left, heading home. He lived in one of the most exclusive neighborhoods in town, at the very top of a hill jutting out off Pontatoc Ridge on the edge of the Catalina Mountains. There were no average homes up here, but George's was unique even for the high foothills. He liked it that way. He pulled into the garage under the house and hopped into the one-man elevator. As he rose to the living area, enormous arched picture windows encircled him. Eagle Eyrie, as he called it, had unparalleled views. To the South, the entire city of Tucson sat at his feet—beyond that he could see all the way to Mexico; to the East, he had a clear, unimpeded view of the majestic Rincons and beyond them the Dragoon Mountains; to the North, Pontatoc Ridge jutted from the Catalinas, with the old Indian silver mine at the top. However, the best view, in his opinion, was to the West. That was, in reality, why he had hurried home. He figured she was due any minute. George turned the lens of his telescope from its focus on the mine and pointed it down to the clear view he had of the picture windows in Misty

Goldstone's bedroom and bath. She wasn't home yet, but he was sure she would be soon.

He knew this path led to ruin, but he ran it anyway, every time. Despite all attempts to stop, he was driven to look, to hurry and wait, to loiter wherever she was. When he was in the heat of it, she was all he could think about. His blood pounded, his heart raced, his face was hot...he was flushed and thick. He lived for that excitement. When he caught her scent, every bit of the dreary day and his more dreary life evaporated in the hunt. He looked again, and saw her dad look out the window. He stepped away from the scope and his heat chilled to ice in a moment.

Now that she was unavailable, he knew he could get some work done. It never occurred to him that who *she* was didn't matter. Sadly, there had been an almost endless string of *shes*, one after the other. Usually *she* just grew too old or faded somehow. Sometimes he got tired of her after he used her. Occasionally though, one would come along that lasted past his first use. Dory had been such a one, but now she was dead, so, it was time to school a replacement. He thought Misty might just do, if he could distract her nosy father. *He should mind his own business,* he thought, *on the other hand, the tighter the fence, the more the bunny struggles to find a hole in the net.*

He walked through his remarkable, if unused, chef's kitchen and pulled a piece of cold pizza out of the Subzero fridge. He looked over the bamboo floors, the massive granite countertops and teak cabinets with disdain. He'd thought this remodel would do the trick, ease the emptiness, fill the void. He knew he'd thought the same thing with the Humvee, the bath remodel, the new floors, even the house itself. Each new thing brought a moment of release, as if this time it would be enough. His constant craving was really satisfied by only one thing. He knew that was not a direction he should go, but he had no way to stop himself.

What I can stop, he thought, *is the relentless snooping into my business by that radio pest, Zane.* His plan to do so was almost complete. He looked over the fake ledger and balance sheets sent him by his tax lawyer. These were copies of the ones he used to explain and hide his income from the IRS. Of course he kept his own records elsewhere. Should anyone get too snoopy, these would quiet the noisiest do-gooder. He'd made the drug business a perfect blind for his real activities. That idiot Zane believed he'd been switching the bales, but when that curtain got pulled there would be nothing behind it. He had pulled only a small amount of cocaine and meth out of the lot in any case, just enough to keep his current coney doped up. Just enough to control her. What little was left he used to set up Spike, the kid he'd used on the Samaniego girls. All his money now appeared to come from very wise and very lucky investments overseas. Only he and Woody knew about the land deals that had netted him the real money. That was the other loose end he had to tie up, but he had that an idea for that too. George was as certain as a man could be that no one would trace through the tangled web of shell corporations that covered his tracks.

His cell rang and he smiled. Problem number two on the line.

"Spike here. Mack told me to give you a call." Mack was Spike's go-between.

"Good you called. We need to meet."

"I'll meet you, but I'm done with selling ... I'm done with you."

"So you've said. I have only one more job for you, and then you can be finished." George smiled again liking his own choice of words.

Spike remained silent for a minute. "Okay, where."

"I can't meet in town, things are too hot." Spike had the nerve to laugh and it pissed off Oldfather. "If I go down, you're going too. Meet me at the RV staging area, Bellota Ranch, past Chiva falls up on Redington Pass, this afternoon at 4:30."

Oldfather hung up and took a quick snort of a line he had cut on the table. He had learned to enjoy a quick buzz occasionally. *I'm not an addict if I don't need it all the time,* he thought. He turned back to the telescope. Just one more look, he thought. Misty's dad was centered in the scope giving him the finger. Not a good omen.

He decided it would be wise to retrieve a weapon from his gun cabinet before he left. It might be a long afternoon and there could be complications.

☼

"Okay, I'll be there." Spike repeated to himself. He'd put the cell back in his pocket, but kept his eyes on the unwitting supervisor. He watched him train his telescope down the hillside and saw where he was looking. *Up to your old tricks.* "Redington Pass, that suits me just fine," he muttered.

Spike knew the area well. He and Dory had met there on several occasions to go hiking and caving. From his perch across the wash and up the mountainside, Spike watched George Oldfather, as a cat would a rat. The super might be a little too large to pounce on, but the idea of putting him in his place was tempting. He thought he had the upper hand for once. The supervisor was still standing in front of the picture window, next to his telescope. He tapped something onto the tall granite table next to him and then pulled out a tube and snorted. Spike could see every detail clearly. This vantage point had a perfect view, yet was unobtrusive. Spike looked down at his feet and saw the cigarette butts of another watcher, realizing others had been here to spy on the super before him. *The man must be stupid,* he thought. *People who live in glass houses, shouldn't get stoned.* He hopped back into Dory's jeep and returned the way he had come, making his way back down the hill. He had a surprise of his own to prepare.

Chapter 18: Repair Work

Woodrow Zapate Madrone sat outside the atrium in his house and oversaw the final corrections and changes requested by the buyers. He shied away from looking at the fresh earth now covering the place where the Samaniego girl had fallen. He couldn't reconcile the conflicting feelings he had about her death. She had been such an enormous pain and inconvenience, yet there was something about her. When George Oldfather had parked her in his house, Woody had assumed it was temporary. It was not. After the first week he'd called George to have him retrieve her, it was too inconvenient. The girl didn't have a vehicle anymore, she'd said, and Woody didn't want to ferry her around. George reminded Woody that he was too deeply entwined with his schemes to refuse this one favor and said it wouldn't be much longer. Woody had decided it might be a good way for him to have leverage on the Supervisor, should he need it. A threat to an official about age inappropriate sex was a powerful thing.

Unfortunately, when George finally came to move her out of Woody's house she'd refused. Later that day Woody kicked her out and locked the door; but the girl was nervy and just broke her way back in. Finally they'd had it out and she produced her claim. He was stunned—and after his encounter with Cory, there was no possibility of asking him for advice. *How had she gotten the deed? Why would Carole Anne have given it to her? How did she know Carole Anne?* The questions had spun around his head while the little puta refused to answer anything. She'd said all she wanted was a temporary place to live. He'd just hoped she would go away— sooner rather than later. As with most things Woody couldn't solve or fix, he stuck those questions in a mental box and moved on. At least she'd spoken good Spanish when she'd wanted to, and she was beautiful.

They'd agreed on a truce, but her presence in his house had still annoyed him. When they argued, he'd toss her out, but she kept coming back. It was a pattern he couldn't break; she'd had a way of making him feel responsible. Then, when he'd caught her in that petty theft. He'd lost his patience, but the girl just produced the deed again and threatened to record it. A claim he'd thought had vanished had come back to plague him. Much as he'd hated to do it he'd tried calling Carole Anne, but when he finally got ahold of her, she just lied, but why? He knew Dory hadn't stolen it but he couldn't think of a reason why she might have given this girl her Estate for Life. Still, he'd never understood Carole Anne. Now the girl was dead and he believed that was the end of the claim, so he should be happy. Instead he felt restless, unable to move in any direction. As with most things in his life he pushed those feelings down. He ignored them, told them to vamos. Usually that worked.

Woody had assumed that after the girl's death the buyers would run, but they stayed. That was when he knew they were hooked. He suspected he could have forced a higher price, but their offer was sufficient. He was also sure he would not have had to fix any of their inspection requests, but he didn't want to take a chance. *This might be my only chance, tal vez es mi única oportunidad*, he thought.

The tradesfolk were all done; he walked through the house inspecting their work and then let each one go in turn. They all knew he would pay them through escrow. None of them were worried; they had all worked for him for years. Now that this distraction was finished, the gnawing ache moved from his heart into his stomach, like a pack rat running to its nest. It made him double over.

He sat down looking through the enormous picture window in the living room to the wonder outside. The desert was shutting down for winter, soon to come. The tiny Palo Verde leaves had turned gold and were dropping. He could see even tinier red leaves on the desert floor. *Otoño en el desierto,* he thought, autumn in the

Page 131

desert was minimalist, Woody's favorite time of year. He saw that the pleats in the Saguaro were tightening up, evidence of no rain since monsoon. A Harris Hawk screeched; he felt empty, aching and sad. Lately, nothing removed this hollowness, neither the magnificence of nature, nor any of his personal work. The world had lost its charm for Woody.

He remembered the invitation to Cory's party, trying to decide if he should let the hard feelings from their earlier blowup pass and just attend. It would be a fitting way to say good-by and fuck off to some of his so-called old friends. He didn't like the way his life had narrowed down recently. It wasn't just that he was getting older and losing people to death—it seemed he'd slowly alienated everyone who had been important to him, one by one. Why? Some said he was too hard and inflexible, but Woody couldn't see any other way to survive.¿Qué esperan? He thought. Apparently his old friends didn't recognize how hard things had been for him. Joy, and good times seemed to be things of the past. The home-building business had gotten tough, almost impossible after the crash. The only way he'd been able to stay alive was to cut wages, fire old workers, cut corners and cheat where he had to.

When Oldfather had approached him to act as a straw buyer for a big land transfer from municipal property, he'd seen it as a harmless way to balance his books and keep alive. Yet what had seemed expedient and harmless had grown to an inevitable and unavoidable trap. Now the heat was on the Supervisor and it wouldn't be long till he got burned as well. If he could just sell this property in time, he could be out the door to...where? Mexico, Taos? Woody guessed the destination didn't matter so much as the timeliness of the exit.

His cell rang, Oldfather. He knew he had no choice but to pick up.

"Hola."

"Woody, glad you picked up. I've got one last thing for you to help me with."

Shit, he thought, *the man never lets up*. "Pendejo! You said we were done."

"After that stunt you pulled at All Souls you owe me."

"Hijo de puta, you son-of-a-bitch. You didn't tell me we were shadowing my ex. And then you pull a gun?"

"It wasn't my gun, I assumed you had fired the shot."

"Well who the fuck?"

"Must have been that geisha bitch you had in tow."

"Besame el culo."

"Yeah, not today. Who was that?"

"Fuck me, I don't know. She just showed up out of nowhere."

"That could be a problem, because there's one more detail we need to fix. After that I think we can both be clear of this mess."

"Which mess, cabron? I think you keep expecting me to clean up your messes. You keep saying this shit."

"The girl, you idiot, the little puta, as you say. Near as I can figure, that is really your mess. Do you want your involvement with me and her to screw up your exit?" Woody understood that Olfather thought he must have had the same intentions with Dory as the Supervisor had had.

"Que, mio?"

"Que...mio. What, poor me you say? You want this fixed, we gotta work together."

"Claro. Háblame, speak to me."

"I've got that kid she used to screw meeting me over at Bellota Ranch, at the staging site above Redington. I want you to come for back up—he might have a bit of an accident."

Woody thought it might be cleaner if Oldfather had the accident, but maybe this would work. "Okay."

"You should come from Oracle, so we can him box him in. He'll be meeting me at around 4:00."

"Si Señor. Te quiero como un niño gordo ama un pastel." Woody loved using Spanish to put asshole gringos that thought they knew Spanish off balance. "I love it, see you there."

Woody stopped by the gun safe on his way out the door. He knew that cabron would be armed and figured he'd better have his own weapon. As far as taking the long way round the Catalina's he wouldn't waste the gas. The supervisor would just have to take what he got.

☼

Oldfather threw the cell on the seat next to him with disgust. He despised Madrone, but he'd always kept his disgust to himself. He knew hiding his feelings kept others useful. *Perhaps Woody's days of usefulness are at an end,* he thought.

Knowing that he had Madrone as back up, he decided a little lunch might be in order. He stopped by La Encantada, thinking it was about time for the rich kids from Catalina Foothills High to stop by. Might as well feast his eyes too.

Chapter 19: A Strange Gift

Spike thought he might need a little protection, so he stopped by his home to pick up the gun he'd nabbed at the All Souls procession. He lived in a small rental over in Menlo Park, the West side of downtown. The house, built in the early '40s, was small, around 900 square feet, two beds and a tiny bath. When he'd moved in, the place had looked like it was falling down. He'd done some drywall and plumbing repair, painted and refinished the floors and planted a little garden. The owner had been delighted and even offset rent for the work. He was proud of his little corner, though he'd never brought anyone home with him. *Perhaps that should change*, he thought, as he opened the door.

He walked into his bedroom and rifled through his sock drawer, pulled out the gun, and sat on his bed to examine it. He'd never used one before, but recently they seemed as common as thorns in the desert, so he'd thought perhaps he should get acquainted. He looked over the weapon carefully, noting that there were three bullets left in the chamber. The metal felt cool, seductive and almost slick in his hand; but it was heavy, a serious tool. He knew little about weapons of any kind, guns least of all. He was amazed he'd had the balls to pick it up. A strange gift from the all souls' angel, he thought.

Spike thought back to the All Soul's event; it was only a week ago though it already seemed like a past life. He'd joined the procession this year because of Dory. She'd always loved it and had gone the previous year with her sister. She'd planned to go this year more to celebrate her sister's life than anything else. She'd needed to bring some closure to the horrible way Mary had died and to her part in it. After Dory died, Spike knew he had no choice but to go for both of them, though he knew now the real reason he'd gone was for himself. A friend had given him a spare mariachi costume and he'd arrived early to have his face painted. At first he felt excited about participating, but things took a different direction when he saw Oldfather adjusting his costume before the parade began.

That was too much for him—the very man he thought most responsible for the death of the Samaniego sisters was there at the parade. Spike realized this might be a chance to get something on the Supervisor and decided to shadow him. When the super met with another player in the drama—Woody Madrone—he knew there was much more going on than he'd thought. Until then, he hadn't even known the two were connected. He only knew Woody from Dory's stay at Scorpion Path. Dory had told him she was staying there because her birth mom had given her some paper or something that gave her the right. Spike didn't really believe it; he thought Woody must have been some other john Dory was using. The men had a brief conversation and then parted. Next, Oldfather met up with another fellow: Mack, Spike's drug connection. Spike realized with a shock how deeply the man had meddled in his life. Till then, he didn't know who Mack worked for.

Mack was dressed up as some hunchback monstrosity, but there was no mistaking that stench. The guy had a stink no amount of deodorant or cologne could mask. Spike knew then that caution was to be the order of the day—thought it was easy to get lost in the crowd and remain unnoticed, so he didn't think he was in any real risk. Soon, however, he realized that the three other men were doing the same thing he was doing to them, shadowing a marcher. He didn't know at first who that person was, under the robes and mask, but he was fascinated with the intrigue...everyone in costume and so many secrets.

For a while he'd become caught up in the drumming, the pageantry and the excitement of the crowd. He'd found himself in the retinue of a man playing the part of Marie Antoinette. Marie's costume was larger than life and her followers held the blue silk train behind him as he walked. His hair was an elaborate beehive with its peak a foot and a half above his head. It framed a picture of a locally famous drag queen who'd died last year from cancer. A few long curls were loose and had been made to trail all around him, floating in the air, as if in a whirlwind. Spike walked under these flowing locks, which were lit from inside and formed a sort of parasol. It was a scene reminiscent of Priscilla, Queen of the Desert. Then, as they approached the final destination and the bonfire, he saw the men again and he wandered in their direction, curious about their intent. When he got closer he saw again the person on stilts. She was reciting a prayer and apologizing to her dead daughter. He knew now who she was—Mary's birth mother, Carole Anne. When Oldfather grabbed her, he got involved. In the melee, a geisha jumped in and brought out the gun. When the shot went off, Dory's mom struck out and knocked the gun away with a kick. People began to panic and run, but the gun stopped by his feet. He picked it up and pocketed it for no reason he could understand. Once he saw she was free, he ran off as well, feeling that in some small way he had helped Dory.

Today, he was glad to have it. He was sure Oldfather had something unsavory planned. Spike needed his own protection. When he'd first started buying drugs from Mack, he thought it was just a business arrangement and a temporary one at that. He hoped selling might get him by, just till he figured out what he was doing in Tucson. Mostly he'd sold to interns at the medical center. That was where he first saw Pari, though Pari hadn't recognized him. One day Mary had asked him about trying a little blow. He'd stopped by the hospital with her in tow, to do a little exchange on the way to a movie. She saw him handing off to one of the docs. That was the day he began to see himself as a pusher.

He realized that had been a big day for him, a turning point. That was also when he'd first run into the Supervisor. Later that night, after he dropped Mary off, he saw Oldfather peeping into her bedroom...not at the glass, but with binoculars, across the street. He'd followed him once he'd left and confronted him, but the supervisor already knew who he was. He said he knew Spike was pushing, he said he'd turn him and Mary in for possession if Spike said anything. Spike didn't have a clue then how Oldfather could have known about the drugs but he thought the Supervisor was serious and it scared him, so he'd agreed. Now it was clear how he had known. Spike felt manipulated and used...he thought he should have called the bluff. If he had, perhaps Mary and Dory would still be here.

That wasn't the worst part about it. After Mary overdosed, Oldfather turned his attention to Dory, and for whatever reason Dory let him have his way. Perhaps Oldfather had played her too, threatening to turn them in if she didn't comply. The worst part was that Spike felt he'd done nothing to stop the mess they'd fallen into. He carried a burden of guilt around for that, and for so many other things. Sometimes the list of things he'd not done but should have completely immobilized him.

Today it was the opposite. Today he resolved to take a stand and begin living his life. He set down the gun, picked up his cell and dialed Pari, expecting to leave a message. He had one prepared, but when Pari picked up he faltered.

"Hello...Spike?"

"Pari, hi. What's up?"

"Ummm, you called me. What's up with you?"

"Hey, I know, just a little tongue tied. Look, I wanted to apologize..."

"Thanks, but for what?"

"Man, for getting you into this mess, with Dory and..."

"You didn't do that, Spike, I'm an adult. What happened wasn't your fault."

"I got the drugs for her, and...." He just couldn't bring up the part about Oldfather.

"I knew that, Dory was a big girl...still, I get it."

"....also I've been wanting to ask you if you want to go out...." He took a breath and waited for Pari's reply. The couple of seconds seemed like minutes.

"Go out. Like on a date?"

Panic set in. *Maybe what happened with us was a one-time thing,* Spike thought. "No, I mean, well, okay, yes...I need some help and I'm hoping you'll go with me right now, I need a hand, your help actually."

Spike was about to blurt out a bit more when Pari answered.

"Yeah. Yes, sure. What and where?"

"Where are you? I'll pick you up, I need to drive up past Chiva Falls."

"I'm at home, at Deels place over on Convent. Text me when you're about here and I'll meet you on the corner."

"Okay, see you in a few." He wondered if he should have mentioned the meeting with Oldfather to Pari but decided there would be plenty of time on the way.

He zipped the gun into an oversized pocket in his leather jacket, locked the door behind him and jumped into Dory's old jeep. It started instantly. *Reliable old Betsy*, he thought remembering Dory's name for the jeep. He'd bought it from her a month before she'd died, meaning to keep it for her, should she ever get clean and need it back. He loved its old lines and solid build, but it really wasn't very practical on a chilly day in November. A northern wind had brought the temperature down. He buttoned up his leathers. Above, silk-ribbon clouds patterned the sky like sand rills on a beach. A sliver moon had just come up...an afternoon moon. It shown through the wisps: a ghost smile through ghost bars. He took a breath, shivered, then flushed. *Everything will be fine.*

Chapter 20: A Sad Waltz

Cory was busy reviewing contract documents in his office; nevertheless he stopped to watch the security window that popped up on his monitor. His security system was smart enough to show him unexpected exits and entries from the building, as well as recording everything to the cloud for safety and ease of access. He watched Pari exit to Church Avenue, open the door of Spike's jeep and get in. He grunted, "Foolish boy!"

His taste for work left him. Normally he was very good about ignoring distractions, but recently his mood was off. He muttered, "Call Evy," his phone obliged, she picked up.

"Boss? What's up? Why'd you call?"

"I did not want to use the intercom. I need you to pull all the info you have—on the land sales, the drugs, the deed...everything. I'll be in the greenhouse. Meet me there in fifteen."

"Sure, thanks Cory!"

He could hear the delight in her tone. Cory knew she'd begun to think all the work she had done had come to naught. She had a subtle but obtrusive way of pouting. He hung up and then spoke to the air again, "Music: greenhouse: 'Valse Triste,' begin in five minutes." That would give him time to listen and reflect before Evy came in. That piece from Kuolema, Sibelius' brother-in-law's play about death might be a bit morose, but it suited his mood and the current concerns.

Cory gave the command to shut down and lock his office systems, then took the hall connecting his office to the greenhouse and his bedroom. He opened the sealed door to the room and took in a deep breath. His nose opened to the damp, pungent aroma of growing plants in mulch. He loved the rich, earthy smell of all greenhouses, but loved his best of all. The scent normally made him feel safe and happy; today, it reeked of the grave. He assumed the good feelings were fostered by memories of his mother dabbling in the lean-to greenhouse his father had built for her in the Dakotas. Why it seemed to be working in reverse today mystified him. Sitting down on the bench near the door he tried to identify the source of his ennui while the Sad Waltz played. Neither the music nor the greenhouse was working. Each made the other seem more artificial and just annoyed him, "Music off!"

He turned the possibilities over in his mind, knowing it wasn't having his ex in the house, nor the absence of his son, nor his young protégé running toward chaos...no, none of these. *What it might be is my inability to find a solution to this puzzle. In turn, I have found fault and guilt with almost everyone involved, but I feel no closer to a solution today than I did a week ago.* At this point he was sure that Pari and Carole Anne were innocent, but that still left Spike, Woody, George Oldfather and even Dolores Samaniego, at the least. Until he'd spoken to Carole Anne, he'd even thought it was possible Dory might have taken her own life. Now it seemed clear someone had a motive to kill, but which motive?

Evelyn came through the door, interrupting his reverie. She had a sour look on her face as she scanned his treasures. She'd told him she thought he was insane to spend time in the desert nuturing his barren, spindly plants. He knew she loved roses and orchids, plants with blooms; she'd let him know that clearly when he had given her a rare euphorbia. "My God," she'd said, "what is that dead thing?" He knew now to give her what she wanted.

The potting table was clean, so she spread out the paperwork on the soapstone surface and began to speak. Cory liked her no-nonsense approach and encouraged it.

"Here are copies of the ballistic tests. Bullets were found from a Smith and Wesson .357 revolver, a Raven Arms .25 semiautomatic"

"The Raven, that would be ours, the gun Pari had?"

"Yes, also a Bryco Arms 9 mm semiautomatic and a Ruger SR9c compact pistol."

"Four different guns?"

"Yes, a bit surprising. We only knew of the guns that Pari and Woody held—the Raven, and the Smith and Wesson."

"The bullet that struck Dory?"

"From a 9 mm, not the guns recovered by the police from Pari and Woody, but the ballistics from the spent casings and recovered bullets identified the two missing makes. Unfortunately, the bullet that killed Dory apparently suffered enough damage before striking her, that most of the scoring on the surface of the bullet was obliterated. Also, because of all the broken windows from the gunshots in and around the atrium, it may be impossible to determine the direction from which she was shot."

"A dead end for us and the police. Any other physical evidence in the house?"

"There was a struggle in the bedroom and two sets of tracks leading away from the house, one heading to Signal Hill, and the other to the pullout before Picture Rocks. There were also signs of a scuffle outside the house and many tracks...too many. Boss, you should look at these documents, the earlier recordings from county land sales that led to the larger sales I mentioned last week. The recordings are prior to the last two years."

Cory had already walked over to look at the ballistics reports on the table, but these recorded deeds told an equally interesting tale. Carole Anne's, Dory's, Mary's and Woody's names were on many of them. Scores of small parcels of land had been assembled to make a few larger tracts which had finally been bought by the county years ago and then recently sold. Something peculiar caught his eye. Cory saw Evelyn smile; she must have deliberately arranged the papers so that he couldn't miss it.

"The notary for every single sale..."

"Yes, I know, it's Dolores Samaniego."

He fanned through the documents and then walked over to the Adenium Arabicum, which was just about to bloom, examining it for any sign of fungus or insects. It was clean. He lightly misted it as he considered the possibilities. This particular plant was one he had bought for Evelyn after learning she hated his thorn forest plants; it was halfway between her taste and his. Right now it just looked like a group of gray yams stuck fat end in the dirt with a few spindly leaves at the top, but when it bloomed it was be a wonder of color and scent. Cory knew she thought it exotic, and he kept it in the greenhouse for her pleasure.

"Thank you Evy, splendid work as always." Evelyn gathered the papers and left, quietly closing the door behind her.

"Music: Greenhouse: Orff: Carmina Burana, two minute start time." Cory looked through the deeds marveling at the tale they told. Years ago, Cory and Dolores had played Go together and as a result, he understood her mastery of misdirection. Yet here was what appeared to be a big mistake. *Unlike her to make this so obvious,* he thought, *unless the trail is laid with intention.*

The music began and filled the room with its magnificent chorus. Cory smiled and, taking in a deep breath, he began potting the new Frankincense cuttings. Their roots were finally strong enough to plant.

His mood had passed.

Chapter 21: In the Dark

Pari knew it was late only from his phone. Nothing had really changed in the cave since they'd entered. *Perhaps it never does*, he thought, *just he same chilly temperature, the same humid atmosphere and the same black-as-pitch, dark-night-of-the-soul light-less hell hole since we arrived.* The only light in the cave was the phone. He was using Evernote on it now to record his journal. It was cumbersome, but it helped him keep calm and he figured he might as well leave a record just in case they didn't make it out. He'd always pushed panicky feelings down by doing something; at the moment he couldn't do much else except work on it. Spike was asleep, and Pari had taken on night watch, a good thing for him, as he was much too keyed up for sleep. *Stuck in a cave...who'd have imagined? Good thing I'm not claustrophobic,* he thought.

He'd decided to pick up where he'd left off, right after he'd visited Scorpion Path with his clients. It was only yesterday, but it seemed like an age ago to Pari. So much had happened he could barely sort it out. He read over the text he'd spent the last hour entering—iPhone spelling corrections had made a mess of some of what he'd written and he wanted to fix them before he continued.

I walked the property with my clients to make sure the atrium glass had been repaired, and to be clear about what requests, if any, they might make as a result of our final walkthrough. We'd finished our list and were on the way back to town. My clients were quiet as we took the last dip and headed up the small incline to the pass over Picture Rocks, but once we crested the hill, the rest of the drive was filled with excitement over the purchase. They acted like kids, as though the house had already closed. Rupert and Dana began an argument over who was going to take care of the atrium, so I stopped them. I felt as though my job at this point was to remind them the deal wasn't done till it recorded.

"Hey you two, the house isn't yours yet. I mean, it's possible that the seller will refuse some or even all of your requests."

Rupert spoke up. "Bloody unlikely, he's already done more than we would have asked. Besides, we'd still buy it even if he refused to do anything." That surprised me a little—but only that Rupert knew it was true and was willing to admit it.

"Well, okay," I said, "but the house still has to appraise and your loan still has to make." Dana spoke up this time.

"You said the appraisal was a shoe in and our lender said we were gold." She was right of course.

"All that may be the case, but a thing isn't done until its done...anything could happen." Like what, I wondered. I turned onto the Interstate and headed back south into town. Dana had been looking perplexed. She had one of those faces that telegraphed everything she was thinking, I could see in the rear view mirror she was getting ready to ask a big question. Finally she spoke:

"So, earlier you said he might not have the right to sell the occupancy of the premises...that Estate for Life thing."

"Right."

"Can we buy the Estate for Life from the person who has it and just deduct that from the sale price?"

"Yes, I think so...maybe you can if they are willing to sell and if the owner is willing to reduce the price by that amount, but I am not sure...I'll ask when we get back"

"Also, what happens if he dies before the closing?"

"Well, I'm not sure, I think it depends, upon whether he has a will or not, I think I should ask Cory when we get back." She sure asked many questions, more questions than I had answers. Then she went on,

"I'm getting a little nervous about all this. I think we need a few answers before we sign final papers...I mean, that is our last chance to cancel the sale, isn't it?"

I admit, I sighed. *"Yes, it is. Remember, we were going to make that final decision after the dinner tomorrow night."*

Pari turned off the phone. In reading the last sentence, it hit home that today was yesterday's tomorrow. The fact that the dinner party was tonight put the fear right back in his heart. *What the hell am I going to do if we can't get out of this hole in the ground?* He felt so panicked he was giddy. Spike groaned and rolled over. Pari turned his phone back on for the light and saw his friend's mud encrusted chest rise and fall. Curiously, that made him feel a lot better. *At least this part of the cave is dry, he thought, it was getting damn chilly in all the mud earlier. We may be dusty but all the mud has dried.*

He admitted to himself that the panic about closing a deal was silly when the real concern was getting out of the cave alive. He took in a few deep breaths, then got back to editing his story.

I told my clients that I'd talked to Cory and he confirmed that,

1) The Estate for Life had been given to Dory (according to her mother) but that it was now lost, so that probably ended that issue.

2) If Woody died, the contract was enforceable on his estate and could not be broken by his heirs, whoever they might be, but it could take some time if we had to go through Probate.

This news calmed my clients considerably, and I dropped them off at their apartment. We resolved to meet the next night, after the dinner to draft our list of requests, or to reject the house should the news prove to be contrary to their interests.

Back at the office, I got a call from Spike—surprising, and exciting. He asked if he could pick me up and give him a hand with something. Of course I agreed. Without even checking in with Cory, I just grabbed my stuff and met him at the corner. I was surprised to see he was driving Betsy, Dory's Jeep, but I was so glad to see him I forgot to ask about it—I just hopped right in and away we went. I wish now I'd told Cory I was leaving. I didn't know where we were going or why, so I don't know how exactly I could have, but I wish I had said something.

Pari now realized how terrified he was.

A noise sounded in the cave, an echoed plop, but in the dark alone in the silence it was frightening to Pari. He turned off his phone for about ten minutes and sat in total blackness. His eyes strained to take in the least light...but there was none. The only sounds he could hear were his own breath, Spike's breath, and his heartbeat. He knew he'd heard something else, but there was nothing now. *God, I wish there were a signal in here,* he thought, looking again for the missing bars. He got back to correcting his entries.

After Spike picked me up, we set off to the East, taking Broadway to Craycroft, north to Tanque Verde Road. Tanque Verde heads up out of the city between the Rincon and the Catalina Mountains and is the only exit to the Northeast. Eventually it becomes almost a four wheel road and traverses Redington Pass. At first we traveled in uncomfortable silence, then, to cover that, Spike turned on the radio, volume up for the wind, and we cruised the roads singing along with Ellie Goulding to "Anything Could Happen." By the end of it we were both laughing and the ice was broken. At a stoplight I turned down the radio and spoke.

"Nothing like a good girlie song to bring up the mood." He laughed. At first I was surprised he was willing to sing such a frothy song, but I was beginning to realize there was more to Spike than leather and studs.

"Yeah, I really like that tune, but don't tell or I'll have to kill you." We laughed again.

"So what's going on, Spike?"

The words spilled out and he told me a lot—how he first saw me, why he started dealing, his relationship with Mary and Dory, how he became entangled with Oldfather and the last conversation they'd had. It was as though he hadn't talked to an adult in years, and I found myself listening with the utmost attention to every word. This man was far more complex and interesting than I could have guessed, and his story stirred me. I could see that, as different as we were, we were also very much alike. We were both normal American guys who people took for something else because of our looks. Spike had tried to change that, going from Kansan-choir boy to its opposite, but really it was just the same thing in reverse. Also, I was feeling something new, kind of warm and full, flushed and excited. Happiness? Kind of a boy crush, maybe. I knew I had to help him, whatever the situation. I looked up and saw we had just passed the Catalina highway and were about to head out on the final leg of our journey. I thought maybe I should reassure him and spoke up at a flashing stoplight.

"I don't think you have anything to worry about with George Oldfather. I mean, he's a county supervisor. If it weren't you telling me I wouldn't even believe he was involved with drugs." I could see Spike had taken in the part about me believing him; he smiled and relaxed at the words.

"That's what anyone would think, but don't underestimate him. He's a great actor when anyone else is around, and he makes sure to reveal himself only when he knows he has something on you."

"So how will he be when you show up with me?"

"That's what I'm counting on...I think we'll be fine. Anyway, I have a bit of a plan. We're supposed to meet at the staging area, but it's way crowded there and I'll suggest going to an area that is a bit more private. Also, I brought a gun."

Neither of these bits of information made me feel any better, quite the reverse. "Wait, didn't you just say he acts different in front of other people? What gun? My experience with guns has been pretty bad recently."

"Look, I won't use it, I'll just bring it out if we need it to give us an edge. Also, the staging area is likely to be empty, but there's no cover and nowhere to go. I've got a place with an escape hatch if we need it."

We sure did.

Another "plop" echoed in the cave sounding very much like a footfall. Pari turned the phone off again and stared into the dark. He finally decided he was just getting the jitters. When the phone was off he didn't hear a thing.

We'd just gotten to the end of the pavement when he finished talking about the gun and the change in venue, so I didn't get a chance to ask him what he meant. I had not been up Redington pass before, so the whole thing was really an adventure for me. The dirt road first plunges down into a wash, which had a little water in it, and then heads up the side of the mountain. The rumble from the washboard, the bumps and grinds from the larger divots and the amazing amount of dust removed any possibility of conversation.

The desert there is gorgeous—saguaros, ocotillos, cholla, and barrel cactus, mesquite and ironwood. Pari pointed out amazing twisted granite boulders in white and grey with veins of orange shooting through them. As we climbed the mountainside, to our right the slopes plunged to a deep canyon, the headwaters of the Tanque Verde. I could see that a little water was flowing through the pools and over small waterfalls far below us. Spike stopped the jeep next to a trailhead. The dust covered us and then blew over in a moment. Spike laughed and spoke:

"Chiva Falls, have you been here?" I shook my head no. "It's a beautiful short hike to the falls, and they really are remarkable. There's a place to swim during the summer...clothing optional." He gave me a bit of a leer. "Not that you would ever. Ha! Anyway, if you come here during monsoon, be careful. Floods come over those falls unexpectedly and people get killed." I must have looked surprised. "Oh yes, and that doesn't count the lost souls who dive off the falls...the pool's not deep enough for diving." With that he put it back in gear and we were off again, up and up and up.

Finally we went through a long traverse and made it over a small rise. The landscape changed from Sonoran Desert to a countryside that reminded me of Wyoming...grass and boulders and some kind of Oak. I'm real sure there were even a few Walnuts. We'd both noticed a truck coming up the pass a few miles behind us. I thought the vehicle looked a bit familiar, but I couldn't place it. Spike said that was to be expected since people came up here all the time for recreation: shooting, off road RVs, camping and even caving.

We arrived at the Bellota Ranch RV staging area; no one was there. Spike pulled all the way in, past the 3 and 4 wheeler loading ramps, to the edge of a dirt track I assumed off-roaders used. He turned off the jeep and we sat for a moment in silence as the dust blew by and the air cleared. A light wind whispered though the trees. I could smell pines, sage brush and cow patties. I could see where a herd had wandered through the area, looking for greener grass. Spike stepped out of the jeep and stretched. I opened my door and had my right foot on the ground when the dirt exploded just a few inches away. I jerked back in the jeep automatically, felt the sting of dirt and gravel on my cheek and heard the crack of gunfire echo off the far peaks.

Spike jumped back in and turned the key...no go! Then a bullet crashed through the windshield on my side, crazing it in a spiderweb pattern just as the motor caught on the second attempt. Spike gunned the jeep and we jerked forward, rushing down the bumpy dirt road.

The next few minutes seemed almost in slow motion. Both of us were so on-edge and aware that it seemed as though we were skiing down the slope, our bodies motionless while the world and jeep careened. We turned through the trees, went up and down a couple of inclines and came out into a long hill heading down to a sandy gulch. The landscape had changed again. There were abundant ocotillos and grey rock...limestone I think. I could see that the four-wheel road plunged right down to the bed of the wash, and that's where we went. Behind us now at the top of the hill I could see two vehicles, a Hummer and a truck after that, the one that had been coming up the pass earlier. Spike shouted at me.

"Shit! I didn't think he'd shoot at us!" He reached into his coat, unzipping a pocket and pulled out a gun. "Here, take this."

"Fuck! What are you talking about? I can't shoot anything when I'm standing still."

"Just take it. I have an idea, but I need you to get my pack from the back and get ready."

"Ready for what?"

"When we hit that bend up ahead, we're getting out. Done any spelunking?"

"No. What?"

"Caving, crawling through holes. I used to do it all the time growing up. Dory and I found this cave up here last year. I don't think they'll follow us, but if they do, we might need the gun...got lights in my backpack."

I grabbed the pack while he rounded the corner in the wash, fish tailing a bit on the sand. Up ahead, a small opening in a bend in the dry creek bed appeared. Spike was going too fast and as he tried to slow down, we slid into the bank and stopped in front of the hole in the wall. The motor turned over roughly, twice, then stalled. I couldn't see the hummer and the truck behind us, but I could hear them. Then they quit too. Silence. The narrowness of the wash must have *been too tight for the hummer. Spike motioned me to follow quickly as he took the pack, jumped out and scrabbled over to the hole.*

Then life stopped for me—it didn't slow, it just stopped. All at once, I was aware of everything around me. It was as if the world had frozen mid-second. I knew it was possible this could be my last breath, last glimpse of the sky. My life didn't flash in front of me—all the world did. Like a freeze frame in a movie, I felt embedded in a picture of existence. The mountains, the trees, each grain of sand spoke to me. The sunset was astonishing. Clouds ribbed the sky like waves on a beach, tinted to soft stripes by the setting sun. That pink glory reflected off the slopes onto Spike's upturned face. For a moment I was the dream, connected to everything, unified......then the crack of gunfire woke me. A bullet jolted the jeep, and then a second. Without a thought more I followed Spike down the rabbit hole into the bowels of the earth.

My eyes adjusted after only a moment, as there was plenty of light filtering through the opening behind us. The hole went down and to my right; here the passage was around six feet wide and four tall, but it narrowed quickly below that. On our hands and knees, we crawled and slid down the slope quickly. The gun shots had continued, most of them hitting the jeep. I smelled gasoline. Light flashed across the walls of the cave followed by an explosion—I felt like my ears were rupturing—and the mouth of the cave collapsed. It was instantly dark, like no darkness like I had ever known. A rush of rock and dirt came sliding over me and I was out.

I'm not sure how long I was unconscious, perhaps only a minute or two, perhaps an hour. I woke up to Spike calling my name and digging me out of the scree. He had a light turned on and looked terrible, dirt sticking to his face where he had been crying. I laughed.

"You look like a raccoon. Rocky Raccoon. I'm okay Spike. What just happened? Where are we and how are we going to get out?"

He laughed briefly, then took a minute to clean me off before he spoke. His expression had turned solemn and I knew we were in a mess. He told me he thought perhaps Oldfather had killed Dory, that he might have been trying to kill us to clean up the loose ends. Then he said he had already checked the entrance looking for me and had seen that it was probably closed for good. He also told me he and Dory had been exploring this cave and another near here the previous year. He thought this cave might connect to the other one they had found over in Beuhman's Canyon.

"That would make sense," he said, "I got a book on the local geology from a fellow caver. It said the sandstone and limestone layers slope down to the canyon and it isn't that far away. Also, Dory and I found water coming out of that cave in Beuhman's last summer. We could tell it was surface water, there was surface stuff in it. I think now it came from this wash, so our best bet is to go down."

And so we went—down and down, through twisting narrow passages that opened onto grottos and rooms with amazing things in them. I had no idea how beautiful caves could be. I saw things Spike described as cave bacon and pearls in pools—unimaginable. I was so entranced I almost forgot we were lost and on the run. Luckily, Spike brought four lights and they have done us well, but after hours of climbing, sliding, walking and squeezing through passages we both ran out of steam. I took a nap first, and now Spike is dozing.

Pari set the phone down. Everything Spike had said couldn't keep his fear, his sense of loss, at bay. He fell into a bit of a reverie, and his morose thoughts wandered. *That glimpse of the sunset yesterday could be my last. I don't want to die full of regrets. I wish I could have been there for Dory. What will my mom and dad think? How can I have let the last words between us be in anger? Then there's Cory. He's such a great man, but I've never told him. He's been like a second dad, but I've ignored his advice and used him. Finally, Spike. At least I can do something about that, but what? I'm in the dark in so many ways.*

The thought about the dark reminded him he still had his phone still on, and he could see the power icon beginning to turn yellow. He shut it off, realizing they might soon need it badly. He sat quietly beside his friend in the dark.

Chapter 22: Boot Hill

At first Woody had followed George Oldfather's crazy driving through the woods and out to this hillside without question, but now he let up on the gas pedal. The area reminded him of Tombstone and specifically Boot Hill, where the unfortunate losers of the OK Corral shootout were buried. He knew Oldfather's Humvee could make it down the incline, but Woody wanted to get out of here in one piece. So he took the truck down as far as was sensible and then walked. Soon, he saw George Oldfather stop his vehicle and get out too, just before he jammed it into that tight little wash. The jeep they were pursuing had squeezed through there, but Woody figured the folks they were following were either stuck or trapped, as he could no longer hear any motor noise.

He watched George peek around a boulder in the wash and saw him begin to fire. He could hear the clang of the impact on the metal of the jeep a bare moment after the sound of the report. They must be very close. Shortly, he made it around the bend in the wash in time to see George Oldfather take his last pot shot at the jeep. George had stepped around the boulder and into the curve, so Woody figured the occupants were either gone or dead. Then the jeep exploded, and the force of it knocked both of them down.

Woody was momentarily deafened and sat up dazed. He watched the side of the arroyo pour down over the flaming carcass of the jeep. In a few moments there was nothing to be seen but a fresh pile of scree sloping down into the wash. Woody thought it might be years before there was enough flow in the arroyo to uncover it again. At the earliest it would be eight months from now, during monsoon, if they had a heavy one, he figured. That was a good thing. No one would have a clue where the jeep had gone.

Clearly this was an unexpected delight for Oldfather who jumped up and began to hop and jig in a ridiculous little dance. He was shouting, or maybe singing: mouthing and gesticulating at him. Woody couldn't tell what the man was trying to communicate because at the moment he couldn't hear a thing. Oldfather's joy disgusted him. He'd had his own reasons to be here, but none of them involved murder. That was how he saw this: murder, another one.

Woody wondered again if the supervisor had killed Dory, or had anything to do with it. He didn't think so but he wouldn't have been surprised. He brushed the dirt, sand and gravel off his behind, noticing that George Oldfather had a piece of Cholla stuck to his pants. Oldfather reached around, without thinking or looking, to brush the little annoyance off of his ass. Of course it stuck in his hand. Automatically, he dropped his gun and grabbed the "jumping" cactus with his other hand. He was trapped...the monkey's paw. This set Woody to laughing, guffawing. Oldfather didn't appreciate that reaction and made his anger known.

"What the fuck are you laughing at? Give me a hand."

Woody thought about it, smiling and raised his own weapon instead. "You can be a son of a bitch, pendejo, when you have your sting, but without it you are just a little niño." George Oldfather went from just pissed off to white hot anger. Woody just laughed all the harder. "¿Quieres ayudar? You want some help? Be more polite before I shoot it off."

"Don't you cross me, you pathetic backwater spic."

Woody laughed again, in earnest. "Or what? Will you trap me with your cactus hands? Claro, que si! You might be right, I am pathetic, but this spic has the upper hand for once. Now, escúchame, listen to me. I don't know who else was in that jeep, but you can hope they won't be missed any more than that little drug using cagada of a boyfriend of Dory's. I'm not unhappy he is gone...because I think he had the deed to my house. No sé en qué otro lugar se. It don't matter a bit because if he did, then no one has it. You should thank the Virgin this mess happened now, in the middle of the week. Because of that, there is no one else up here to see, except me. But I saw. I saw you kill that little maricón. Now, let's have a little conversation about el futuro, the future. Tu quieres, you want my silence? Well, you can have it, if you never call on me again."

Woody saw Oldfather was trying to ignore his disadvantage. Woody had learned that the man was nastiest when he didn't have any advantage, but he was also more manageable. Woody laughed again—that pathetic man kept looking for anything that might give him a leg up. He decided there was no reason to ask who the other person in the jeep was. He figured Oldfather knew, but the less Woody knew the better. Madrone was many things, but an actor was not among his talents and he was aware of that.

"Agreed. You know, once this day passes, you'll go down with me if you say anything. You are going to Cory's dinner, I assume?"

"Yes, I want to go, and I think we must both go."

"We need to leave here from different directions, and not the way we came."

"Es Cierto esso. Yes, I agree. I will take the route around to Oracle, back to Picture Rocks. You should go through Benson."

Oldfather nodded.

Woody frowned and spoke again. "Do you think there is any chance they are alive?"

Oldfather laughed out loud, but winced, as he inadvertently drove the thorns in a bit deeper. "Take this piece of shit cactus off my hands!"

Woody pulled a comb out of his pocket and deftly removed the teddy-bear cholla from the Supervisor's hands.

George continued, "Nothing could live through that, and there's no way out of that hole they crawled into."

Woody thought that was probably true. Nevertheless, he thought they should err on the side of caution and camp here the night. George didn't like the idea, but as he was protesting, a bit of scree fell away and exposed a fender. So, Madrone set about gathering wood for a fire while Oldfather shoveled more scree down the slope. He figured the fire would explain the earlier smoke, should anyone be coming this way. George had some MREs in the Humvee he doled out for dinner. Oldfather slept in his vehicle, Woody in a sleeping bag he kept in his truck.

In the morning, George backed the vehicle out of the wash under Woody's direction and then drove him up to his truck. From there they took a diversion off the RV trail to an old mining road, currently out of use. This led them back to the main dirt road heading out to the San Pedro Valley. Woody headed out first, so there was little chance of the two of them being seen together.

Woody watched George in his rear view mirror until he saw him start down the road and turn in the other direction. He knew the man was fully capable of putting the gun to further use, and he was prepared to gun the motor at the first sign of anything odd. He wasn't too worried, though; the dust was so thick it would have been hard to get off an accurate shot. Nothing happened, so he made his way northwest, behind the Catalina Mountains on the road toward Oracle. He enjoyed traveling on these rough back roads, it put him back to his youth. For a moment, crossing the deep wash coming out of Beuhman's Canyon, he thought about taking a hike up that slot to where he remembered water coming out of a hole in the wall...a cave exit he supposed. He used to take his girls up there in the summer for a little skinny dip in the slot canyon, and then gave them something else to warm them. That little waterfall pouring out of the slot wall always did the trick. Got the little putas cold so he could heat them up again. He smiled at the memory and drove on.

☼

Oldfather wished he'd been able to orchestrate the cave-in a bit better...his ideal would have been to have Woody follow those two down the hole and then whoosh! End of problem. Instead he would have to navigate a few more tightropes before he could escape the glare of public attention and his unmasking. Once he saw Woody disappear down the road to Oracle, he turned around and headed back to Redington pass. *Damned if I'm going to take the time to go all the way back through Benson*, he thought. The other reason, of course, was that George Oldfather trusted no one. He thought it was possible Woody might turn around at the last moment. He wouldn't let the back of his head center in anyone's gun sights. He started to worry over the bullets and casings left back at the scene. He figured it unlikely that anyone would find anything identifiable, but on a whim he veered near the edge of a steep cliff on the road and tossed the weapon out the window.

He was happy with the toss. *Went right into the arms of that saguaro*, he thought. He rolled up the window and popped in the CD of New Found Power by Damageplan. He listened to Lachman scream out the Words: "Cleansing yourself from the past" and almost joined in. *God, I love heavy metal.* The former singer from Pantera wailed, his voice sounding like a pig being slaughtered. *A pity Dimebag got shot, but what a way to go.*

Chapter 23: Claustrophobia

Carole Anne thought she was coming unglued. She needed wide open spaces. Even storing clothes in a closet made her short of breath. When Cory had mentioned staying in the "safe room," she hadn't realized it meant being locked up in such a tiny space. *Like money in a safe,* she thought. There wasn't even a window, and she couldn't figure out how to unlock the door. *Sure, it's all for my protection, but shit!*

She was okay at first. She'd slept, watched a movie, taken a light snack from the fridge, sat, walked in circles—it got old fast. Also, she was beginning to regret the recent conversation with her ex. Not that she didn't want to reconnect, and not that his help wouldn't be useful—and it was good to be back in his circle—all that was okay. No, she needed to be free and to do things on her own. She was nervous about what might happen next. Not being in control of her own situation when the dice did roll was intolerable. The last thing Carole Anne needed or wanted was for some man to come in and fix things, least of all Cory. *No, and no again.* She needed to breathe. She needed to get out, but how? To her relief, there was a knock on the door.

"Carole Anne?"

Thank God its Evy and not Cory, she thought. "Come on in!"

Evy opened the hidden door and Carole Anne noted how the decorative clavos in the center of the false panel moved—one after the other just before the door opened—she could do that. Evy entered with a breakfast tray. *Cory's idea of breakfast,* Carole Anne thought. Genoa salami, Jarlsberg cheese, his homemade olives, a few apricots, a flask of coffee and one of wine, preserves and a baguette. *Perfect traveling food,* she thought. Evy looked a bit harried.

"Thanks for breakfast." Carole Anne smiled.

"Oh sure, you know Cory, always needs to feed people. Will this work for you? I could bring something more traditional." She fumbled with the tray, nearly dropping it before setting it on the small table near the TV.

"Nah, this will be fine. What's the matter Evelyn?" Carole Anne thought this might be a good time to pump her for a little information.

"Nothing, really, or I think nothing. Cory asked me to give Pari a call, to have him drop by a store for some dinner ingredients—he's not answering his phone."

"He's a kid, probably turned it off."

"Well, maybe, but I don't really think that's it. You see, we have a software tracking program on my workstation. It knows the GPS signals of all the agent's phones and it records where they are."

"Wow, that seems sort of big brotherish."

"Well, I guess so. The agents like it because if they lose a phone I know exactly where it is, within a few feet...and if they have any problem while they are showing houses or at an open house, I can send the police to their exact location. Also, the records are admissible by the IRS for travel expenses."

"Okay, I guess that is cool."

"So, Pari's phone winked out just on the other side of Redington Pass."

"Perhaps he's out of range."

"Nope, this system is not cell phone signal dependent, it's a GPS satellite function."

"Okay, well that may be true for the receiver, but not for the signal going out of the phone."

"How do you know that?"

"I have a GPS system on my bike, but I wanted to be sure I couldn't be tracked, so I did some research. Trackable devices receive from the GPS satellites, but have a separate system that sends a pulse out through radio, over cell phone frequencies or with the best ones to communication satellites. So he could be out of range for any of those."

"Got it. Still, the signal over the pass must be strong now because I have a couple of agents who sell in the San Pedro and I can track them. Sometimes the signal goes away as they switch towers, but it always comes back. Pari's been out of communication for a while. I'm thinking of taking a drive over Redington just to see if I can find him."

"Did he go alone?"

"No, he went with that Spike fellow."

"Spike Smith?"

"Yes, they're friends."

Carole Anne thought on this for a moment. "Spike and I had some words about Dory. I even thought he might have been the one at the time."

"The one?"

"The one who killed Dory."

"Wow."

Carole Anne didn't mention that the words they had were at the parking space off Scorpion Path on the day Dory had been killed, or that Spike had been there to pick Dory up after she retrieved a few more of her things from the house. She remembered how shocked she'd been to see Spike driving Dory's jeep, Betsy, the one she'd bought her daughter. She couldn't forget how rude he had been to her and how he'd called her a bitch for abandoning Dory. She'd slapped him and he'd driven off in a fury, after telling her he didn't need any more shit from either of them and that she ought to go pick up her daughter and take care of her. "That's what a real mother would do," he'd said.

She hadn't mentioned that to anyone, nor the fact that she had stayed at Scorpion Path until later. *Later that day, the day my daughter died,* she thought. *I have secrets—me and almost everyone else; everyone has a secret or two.* She didn't mention the other arguments she'd had that day, with Dolores and Woody, or the gun she had lost. Why would she? She noticed Evy examining her and realized with a shock that this woman thought she might have killed her own daughter. So she cut the tête à tête short.

"Well, thanks for the chow." Carole Anne gave her best "good friends" smile.

"Listen, I have to go, but I wanted to tell you that I moved your bike off the street and over to the Ramada in front of the office, where I can keep an eye on it."

Useful information, Carole Anne thought. "Thanks Evy, can I call you that?" *Perhaps a little too sweet, better tone it down.*

"Yeah, I like Evy a whole lot better than Evelyn. Too bad my boyfriend can't figure that out."

"Just tell him, Evy. Men are dumb fucks. They don't know anything unless you tell them. That's what I've learned."

Evy laughed. "I think you're right."

"I know I'm right. So you're going to drive over Redington Pass?"

"Just to the location Pari's phone went out, unless I hear from him first. I'll be back by this afternoon—I have a lot more to do, but that little bugger Pari, he's got under my skin."

"Is that a good thing, or a bad thing?" Carole Anne asked with a hint of irony and a laugh.

"Oh, good. I think he's going to be a great addition to out team once he gets his feet." With that Evy closed the door.

Carole Anne got to work almost immediately, pulling her pack out from under the bed where she had stowed it and shoving in the few possessions she had with her. She looked at the tray and then pulled out a Ziplock from a side pocket of the pack. *Ziplocs and a towel, almost all you need for a road trip, besides your bike and leathers*. She drank the coffee and dumped the food, without ceremony or order, into the Ziploc and stowed it. She took a sip of the wine and dumped it down the sink in the bathroom, filling it instead with the filtered water Cory had coming out of the tap. *Tastes insipid, but it's wet*, she thought. Carole Anne liked regular tap water far better than anything coming from a bottle or an osmotic filter. Next, she moved the clavos on the door in the same pattern she had seen earlier and, presto, the panel opened.

She slipped out the door into the hall and, gently closing the secret panel behind her, quickly made her way to the garage. Of course the motorcycle wasn't parked in there. It was outside, in front of the brokerage. She peeked through the spy-hole in the door leading out from the garage to be sure Evy had already left. The coast was clear, and in a moment, Carole Anne was on her way. She'd decided a ride around the Catalinas from Oracle was a good idea. It would clear her head. If, by chance, she came upon Dory's old jeep, she figured it would be just fine to stop them and let them know to turn on the phone. Besides, she just might locate that deed and retrieve it from Spike.

☼

Cory watched Carole Anne drive away on his security monitor—much as he had watched her leave so many times in the past, always with mixed emotions. Having listened to the conversation between the two women in the safe room over that same security system, he had a very good idea where she was going and why. *Good, I can use her resources, as well as Evy's, to locate Pari and get everyone here for the party,* he thought. If the deed was produced, so much the better. It was a risk for her to go off on her own, but he'd placed a GPS bug on the bike, so he would know where she was.

Chapter 24: Through the Rabbit Hole

Spike woke up to the sound of fingers on a phone and the gray light of a smart-phone screen reflected off the dusty formations on the wall beside him. His immediate reaction was to lash out at Pari for wasting the power and the light. He knew the possibility they might escape this branch of the cave system had almost vanished yesterday. He'd needed the sleep because he had worn himself out, desperately trying to find the connecting route he was sure must be here—somewhere. It had also been exhausting keeping up a cheerful and positive front for his friend when what he really felt was unbridled terror. *Perhaps it's better to let Pari occupy his mind filling in the details in his journal*, he thought; after all, Spike was no stranger to compartmentalizing his own fears. Sometimes that was the only way to get through the day.

He took a mental inventory of their situation: 1 liter of water, two granola bars, some rope, two flashlights almost finished and two more with a couple hours of power left between them, his phone already out of power, Pari's phone, with who knows how much remaining power, a Swiss army knife, a pack and a gun...what a lot of help that had been. Spike had brought them to a dry portion of the cave to rest, but it was a cul-de-sac. He'd led them here after the passage he was pursuing narrowed down to a rabbit hole. He now realized that was the only possible way out, but he wasn't sure if it was big enough for them to fit through, and it was wet, very wet. *What if I get down there and it's flooded and I can't back up? What if Pari isn't up to it? What if, what if!* He turned around and Pari spoke.

"You're up! What's next boss? I tried to keep awake, but I confess that I fell asleep for a few hours. Just woke up myself, it's 6:30 AM."

Good God he's cheerful; I'd better keep him that way, Spike thought, but then realized Pari might be a better help if he knew the score. "Well, a little breakfast first." He broke out the granola bars and opened the water.

"Shouldn't we reserve some of that?"

"Nope, better to have the energy and the fluids in our bodies, we'll need it for the next push." He took a deep drink and then handed the bottle to Pari. "We need to backtrack a bit, back to the rabbit hole I found yesterday."

"I thought you said that probably didn't go."

"That's what I thought at the time, but Pari, none of the other branches goes either, so I think we have no choice." He could see Pari take it in. "Here's my thought, we're going back there and I'm going to try the hole. I'm going to try to make it through. If I make it I need you to follow me."

"Try? Do or do not. There is no try." In spite of the situation, Spike laughed at Pari's imitation of Yoda.

"Okay, I get it, but this is serious. We'll tie the rope to my foot. If—no, when—when I get to the other side I'll pull three times. That means I've made it and you must follow. If you don't get the tugs, you have to go back to the beginning, because that will be your only chance at that point." He heard no response and figured this had hit Pari very hard. "Look, I think our chances are good, but we have to be prepared for the worst. Also, we need to get a move on. I think we don't have that much time left on the flashlights."

In the phone's light, Spike saw Pari nod and without any further conversation they gathered up their meager possessions and set back on the way they had come. It took them an hour to get back to the rabbit hole. The situation looked doubtful to Spike, and he couldn't imagine what Pari was feeling. The first two of their four lights had died and they'd already switched to the remaining pair. Spike suggested they pack the used up lights and anything else they didn't need in the rucksack and leave it. Pari told him he was real uncomfortable with that idea and looked near a panic attack. In truth, Spike didn't like it much either.

Spike examined the path he was about to take. The hole curved down and narrowed until it was just barely big enough for him to get his shoulders through. The only way for him to do it was to go headfirst, arms in front of him, holding one of the lights. Spike had done this before, but decided it might be a good idea to explain what to do and what might happen to Pari in detail. Pari listened to the whole thing, and showed his panic only when Spike mentioned going through water.

"What do you mean, go through water?"

"I won't send you through it unless it's just a dip, but there is a chance this hole goes through water before it comes out into the next room. I'm telling you, you need to just go through if you come to water, take a breath and go, but go quickly."

"Wow."

"Trust me, Pari. If you can't make it I will pull four times, and that means I'm okay, but you should head back to the place we came in. I will head on from there and come out in Beuhman's and I'll be back for you." He knew this sounded hollow.

Spike decided to take a few minutes resting before setting out and they sat together in the dark. Pari's hand found Spike's and the two of them sat like that together listening only to each other's breath for several minutes.

Finally Pari spoke, reciting lines from a poem Spike knew but had long forgotten.

"I wake and feel the fell of dark, not day.

What hours, O what black hours we have spent."

"Hopkins" Spike said, "But I admit, not my favorite of his poems."

Pari laughed. "Mine either, but that line came to mind."

"Okay, but how about this instead:

"And though the last lights off the black West went,

Oh, morning, at the brown brink eastward, springs..."

Pari sighed, "That is better, morning always comes after a long night...it's from 'God's Grandeur,' I think."

Spike nodded and then laughed at his unseen body language. "You're right, but how did you know that?"

"My Indian parents sent me to a Catholic grade school. I even went to mass sometimes. That's where I learned about Gerard Manley Hopkins—I had to memorize and recite several of his poems as punishment." He laughed. "Until now I haven't know anyone else familiar with him...It's kind of strange that we both know the same obscure poet. It seems like a sign or something."

"It's not just strange, it's weird—I don't know any other guys that know any poetry. Odd thing—Mary, Dory's sister, introduced me to Hopkins. She'd discovered him in a lit class when we were dating; she'd had to prepare one of his poems to read, the one about Margaret...Spring and Fall to a Young Child. I helped her memorize it. I read the rest of the book and found out I liked his stuff."

"Some of his poems are awesome, but you have to read them out loud to hear it."

"That's what got me, hearing Mary say some of those lines out loud. When she came to the line: It is the blight man was born for—I nearly wept—wow, it kind of shakes me up thinking of that and how easily life can slip away."

Both of them were silent a moment before Pari spoke. "Spike, I know this might seem odd to you, but in my whole life I haven't felt closer to anyone than I do to you. Kind of pathetic, I guess. Still, in this moment, I want you to know you are really important to me. I don't want you to go down that hole without knowing it."

Spike pulled Pari closer and gave him a long hug. He could not remember feeling this close to another person either. "We've got lots more to do, you and me." Then he kissed him, and for a moment the separation between them vanished and neither knew where the other's lips began or where theirs ended. "Let's get out of here."

With that, Spike tied the rope to his foot and he made his way down the hole.

☼

In a minute, too soon, Spike was gone and Pari was left with one flashlight on, and the rope playing out, pulling through his palm, stedily. The rope was long, Pari guessed around 25 feet. That had seemed like a lot to him when he was imagining where that hole went...but the coils kept disappearing, and the rope kept pulling through his hand, moving down through the hole, inch-worming in a maddening crawl as Spike's foot pulled it ever further.

Pari kept anticipating the tugs from Spike, hoping they would come, but they didn't—just the slow pull. Three times the progress stopped. Each time Pari waited for the tugs from Spike. Each time after a few agonizing minutes the rope started moving again, further down the hole. How far did the hole go? Finally, the end of the line was in front of him, and Pari watched with panic as the end pulled into his palm.

He leaned forward into the slope, and then lay down in the hole, following the trailing rope. He started to slip and moved to readjust his purchase, but in a moment the rope slipped from his hand and disappeared down the hole. In his panic he dropped the flashlight, which went out as it fell down the rabbit hole. He felt around, panicking in the dark, with no rope, no flashlight, nothing. He scrambled back up the slope, as if death itself waited for him with an open, dark mouth. Pari was alone. He looked around wildly, or tried to. He listened, straining eyes and ears for any light or sound, but there was nothing.

Alone, in the dark, in the silence.

Chapter 25: The Game of Go

Cory looked with satisfaction at the seating arrangement in the dining room. The table itself, carved out of Peruvian mesquite, was massive, 6 feet wide and 16 feet long. It would have dominated most dining rooms, but looked appropriate in this one. Cory could easily accommodate eighteen, but tonight's dinner for eleven gave each guest ample space, as well as plenty of room for everything else. He'd thought carefully about the seating arrangement, placing himself at the head, closest to the kitchen, of course. On his right, were name cards for Evelyn Valdez, George Oldfather, Carole Anne Michaels, Woody Madrone and Spike Smith. Evy would sit right next to him, both so she could help serve and so she could hem in the men on that side of the table, closest to the wall.

He'd placed Spike at the end because he was the least threat and more likely to act as a barrier to the others. On his left were name cards for Pari Workingboxwalla, for Pari's clients Dana and Rupert Brooks, Dolores Samaniego, and Officer Philip Moreno. Cory figured Officer Moreno could be trusted to handle an end run by any of the three men opposite and could also deal with Dolores, should she end up being a problem. *Seating arrangements are very important in planning a party,* Cory thought. He had always held that anticipating conversation and guests' actions could make an evening unforgettable. *However,* he thought, *when the guests have issues with each other it is much like placing the first stones in the game of Go.* Still, he wondered what would happen if someone failed to show up.

He'd sent Evy a text asking her if she had found Pari, but the answer was no, as of yet. That concerned him. He brought up the GPS tracer ap on his cell and saw that Carole Anne was just passing Oracle. At least the two of them would complete a loop. He wondered if perhaps one of his other guests had planned this diversion. The absence of Pari and Spike would be a clever distraction. This brought his thoughts back to Dolores's RSVP, which

Evy had so carefully repeated word for word. "I would love to play a game with him some time, if he has finally learned about ladders," she had said. Indeed, he had learned. But what could be done if one of his stones was missing or out of place?

Cory had first learned to play Go more than twenty years ago, from Dolores Samaniego, who had grown up in an orphanage in Japan. One of her caregivers had taught her the game. She was a good teacher; her instructions were simple and had stayed with him to this day, though back on the base it had been anything but simple.

It was a long time ago, but seemed like yesterday...he was about to knock on the Samaniegos' door, in the middle of deciding what story to tell them. Cory needed to cover the fact that Carole Anne had not come to dinner with him. They'd had an argument over money—over their very different ideas on when and where to spend it. The fight came to a head when Carole Anne, taunting him, had mentioned that his new business partner, Woody, didn't mind spending money on a good time. Cory had said words back to her, words he regretted, and Carole Anne had told him to "fuck off" and go on without her. "I'd just as soon spend my evening working on my bike as sit there with Dolores and Hernan faking a good time with you," she'd said. At this point he didn't want to be here either. He wasn't up to faking it and would have preferred to nurse his wounds alone with a drink. He'd just decided to leave and call them later when he heard someone inside.

Dolores opened the door, alone, and invited him inside without mentioning Carole Anne's absence. He walked into the living room, expecting to see Hernan sitting by the TV with a beer, but his seat was empty. Cory turned, hearing Dolores clear her throat. She was standing, back to him at the front door, slowly closing it. Snick went the latch as she slid the bolt.

"Hernan was called in to work the night shift, one of his coworkers is sick."

They shared a moment of awkward silence and then Cory realized it was his turn to speak. "Oh, sorry, too bad." Cory said, wondering why she hadn't turned back to face him.

"What shall we do—you without Carole Anne and me without Hernan?" she asked, still facing the door.

Cory was feeling increasingly uncomfortable. He found Dolores quite attractive and knew the feeling was mutual, but they had never acted on it. Nevertheless, sexual energy colored their every conversation, as few as those were. He was friends with Hernan and couldn't betray that trust, but until now it had been an easy task, as he and Dolores were never alone.

"I don't know, maybe I should just go?" He asked this in a tone that insured she would tell him to stay.

"Why?" she finally turned around to face him, "We are both here and we both must eat. I've cooked."

Cory looked around the apartment as if searching for a place to sit, stalling for time. Sweat broke out on his forehead, delicious and forbidden desire stirred. Finally he noticed the game board set up on the coffee table.

"What is this game? I've always wanted to ask you about it."

Dolores exhaled. *All the emotion she will allow herself,* Cory thought. The restraint doubled his interest. She moved into the room, gliding more than walking, as if she had no feet, but only rollers under her dress. In other people this would have been comical, but Dolores pulled it off.

"It's called Go. It's an ancient oriental game of strategy and cunning. I've been trying to teach Hernan, but he has little interest."

"I would love to learn, if you will teach me."

She smiled, a rare event, and nodded. "The game is easy to learn, but takes a lifetime to master"

"I have a lifetime," he returned the smile, "and we have time now."

"I agree. However, this game on the board cannot be disturbed. I am playing it with my old teacher, through the mail. So I will have to teach you the rules on paper."

"That is fine, I love being a student. Will there be a test?"

"Most certainly."

He already liked this game.

She hid a smile and pointed to the game in progress. "Play is on a board of intersecting lines. We play the intersections, not the squares."

"How many lines?" he asked.

"Nineteen, like this board, though you can play a smaller one. Each player has an unlimited number of stones, white or black.

Page 183

Black plays first. Players alternate, one stone at a time on any free intersection. The object is to occupy as much real estate as possible."

He had gone right to the point of the game, "Can you capture your opponent's stones?"

"Yes, if they do not have the space to live. To live, they must have a liberty, an open line. Stones are connected through the lines, not diagonally, and if one is alive, all the connected stones live. The exception to being able to play anywhere is that you cannot play into a space surrounded by other stones, unless playing into that space captures the other stones."

"I confess, I am a little confused."

"Let me show you. Here is an example."

She swept the stones from the game in progress, then spread a sheet of plastic wrap over the board, placing four black stones down and six white ones. She then marked positions on the grids, to demonstrate the basics.

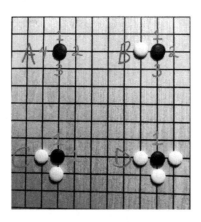

"You are black. In A you have four liberties, in B You have three because I have removed one with my stone. In C you have two liberties, but in D you only have one, and if I were to play there, I would capture your stone."

"In D, none of your stones are connected, so each one of them has three liberties."

"That is correct." She said, "Now look at this configuration." She swept the board again, carefully marking each position. Cory marveled at her passion for the game.

"Here, your stones are all connected and they have five liberties between them, but my stones are in two groups."

"Yes, I see that," said Cory "Your two groups are each of two connected stones and both groups have four liberties."

"Yes, very good. Now, look at this scenario."

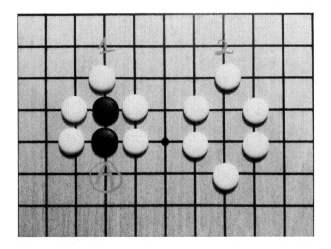

"If I were to play at space A in example one, then I would capture your two stones, as I have shown in the second example."

"But after that, could I play into one of those spaces?"

"You could, but it might be a pointless sacrifice, as I would immediately play into the other space capturing your stone."

"And is there any other way I could play into the single space left?"

"Yes, but only if it captured a group of stones, and changed the game. If that capture is a repeat of an earlier pattern, it is forbidden. Here, take a look at this group."

"Ah, we could take each other's stones forever."

"Yes. You can see that I could take stone 1 by playing in the red circle, but then you could play back to stone 1 ad infinitum. That is why there is a special rule, the Ko rule, which does not allow you to make a move that returns the game to a previous position."

"I've got it."

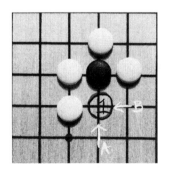

"Now, let's talk about ladders. You must understand them to play strategically. Look at this example.

Starting from this situation, it might not seem that the black stones are trapped, after all, if you play in position one they have two breathing lines at A and B.

However, if you played a stone number one at position a, then I would play my stone to block at position 2, then you must play yours at 3 to escape, as below.

It is easy to see that move 11 by you, connecting to stone 9, would be the only way you can save your group. However it is also easy to see that it is a temporary save, as I would just play 12 diagonally from 8. If this chain continues to the end of the board you will lose all your stones once I play at 18, as below."

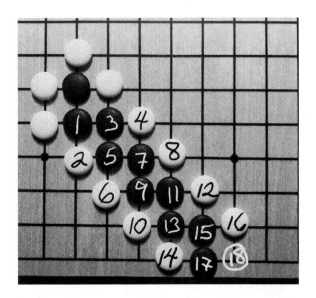

"Yes, I do see that, because they would not have a liberty."

"However, if you had already played a stone ahead of this ladder, they might live. And, if I have also played ahead of this ladder, I might capture the group anyway."

Lost in this remembrance, he was totally unaware of the person who had entered the dining room and had walked up behind him. She touched him on the shoulder, and he jumped. He turned to see Dolores Samaniego looking over the name cards on the table.

"I see you do seat people strategically at your dinners." Dolores turned to him and smiled. "Evy let me in, I hope that's okay."

He nodded, marveling again at her icy yet magnetic beauty. Her smile, though apparently genuine, did not convey what she felt, he knew. Dolores had all the best qualities of Anglo and Asian features: creamy complexion, almond eyes with flecks of green, high cheekbones and silken hair. Age and sorrow had only deepened her exotic elegance, yet there was something hard and cold to her. In all the years he had known her, she had never shown her real emotions. She was a master of misdirection and her smiles often hid deep anger while her disinterest indicated the opposite. Indeed, Cory had found the degree of apparent disregard directly indicative of her true desire. He knew that under her smooth, cool exterior she was fire incarnate. Despite himself, Cory had always found her deeply attractive, but over the years they had both used that attraction in their games together, rather than consummate it in any physical release.

She spoke again. "Cory, I hardly think you need to remove one of my liberties with Moreno. Who is Rupert Brooks?"

"Rupert is one of my agent's clients. He and his wife are buying Woody's house. The house where Dory died."

She appeared to take this in. "Thank you for having this wake, though it is really not my style."

Page 189

"I know that"

"So I can assume you have several other reasons for this gathering." Cory saw that she had noted the card set out for Supervisor Oldfather.

"There are other reasons for this gathering, it is true. However, any reason not having to do with the death of your girls and the sale of this house, should only work to your advantage."

Dolores now knew the focus of the evening was not on her activities with Oldfather, but she needed to be certain. "So there is more afoot here than I thought. I should have suspected. Perhaps Moreno's presence here is appropriate."

Cory suspected she was aware of all this already, she continued. "So I take it I am also part of your game with the clients and Woody? Yet, there must be something more, or the Supervisor would not have been invited. I assume you have me seated across from that remarkable man for another reason." Her sarcasm was uncharacteristically revealing to Cory.

"Yes, he must be contained, and you are the one person able to cast that net."

"Indeed." She smiled a particularly chilling smile. "If I am I to be one of your stones, you must take me into your confidence, otherwise my play will be unpredictable." Cory knew she was already playing the game, testing him to see where she fit on his board, or if he had brought her here for a killing stroke.

"Ah, you are here to prevent a ladder escaping from the other side of this board, from anyone opposite, no more, no less."

Page 190

"So then, this is not our game?" He knew she might mean the opposite, but play had begun and he kept up the thread.

"No, Dolores, we may have another game to play later, but on this board we are not competitors." Her face remained implacable as she responded.

"How sad."

Chapter 26: A Flash of Light

Pari finally fell apart in the dark. He'd put on a show with Spike, pretending that everything was okay, but he was scared. Now he was alone and hopeless even though Spike had gone bravely forward or maybe because of that. Then he saw a glow—light! It was coming from the phone in his pocket. He pulled it out to see a text message from Evelyn asking where he was. *Damn if that doesn't put a whole new perspective on things,* he thought. It improved his mood tremendously, until the battery died, he was in the midst of returning her text when it failed. Instantly plunged back into night, he freaked again. The good thing was it made him realize he might be closer to the surface than he thought, and it gave him the hope to move. He had nothing to lose by going forward and nothing to gain by staying still, so without thinking about it he plunged into the hole. It was terrifying, but at least he was doing something.

The hole sloped down almost 45 degrees at the beginning and then began to level out a bit as it narrowed. At first he was slithering down more rapidly than he wanted, but he stuck out his elbows and slowed the slide. The mud here was sticky and thick, and it stunk—he realized it must be bat shit. The knowledge was oddly comforting. He figured if bats had been here to poop, there must be a way out. Then, feeling around in front of him, he felt the flashlight, but in his excitement he knocked it down further into the hole. *Never mind*, he thought, *I'm going that way anyway.*

He began humming in the dark to the tune of "Working in a Coal mine" as he wiggled forward, and with every "whoop" he'd give an extra push. He was surprised at how soon his hand grasped the flashlight and with a shout he turned it on. He almost wished he hadn't as he could see ahead that the hole sloped down again, and sharply. He could tell where Spike had passed before him, and where the rope after Spike had left its trail. What was worrying him was the trickle of water pouring out of a side tube into this one.

That, and the reflection of his light off the surface of the water covering the hole below.

He stopped there for a few minutes, catching his breath, or trying to. He was so scared he was beginning to hyperventilate. Pari decided to try to turn around, or back up. After a few futile attempts he realized backing up was simply not possible. Finally he moved forward, down to the water. It was cold, freezing cold. It had been clear at the top, because of the new flow slipping into it, but his uncertain progress had sent a flurry of mud into the stream and now it was mostly opaque. He put his light into the muck to see if that might help illuminate where he would be going, but that was a mistake. The seal in the tool must have been loose, because not a moment after he submerged it, the light blinked out.

Before this, he had not imagined he could be so scared and desperate. *Trapped in a cave, no way out, what can I do?* He wondered. He'd already cried out, had no more tears, and his hysteria was gone too. All that was left was the cold, the dark and the sick feeling of certitude. *Frozen, black inevitability, that is the scariest feeling of all,* he thought. *My options are all gone except the one I fear the most.*

He knew he had to go down through that hole, but he could not bring himself to begin. Caught in this terrible dilemma: fear of death if he stayed and fear of death if he continued, he began to shiver. The shivering became so intense it was really a case of rigers, the kind of shivering that shakes a person off the bed. He had seen this once when someone came into the emergency room with Dengue fever, one of the worst tropical diseases. The shivering itself scared him. *Knowing what something is does not rob it of its power,* he thought. He began to slide forward, he couldn't stop himself, and knew he had no choice but to continue. He took a breath, and called on the all the names of God he knew: Ram, Krishna, Shiva, Allah, Jehovah, Zoroaster, the Buddha. He called every name of God he could remember, hoping for any help. Then he plunged into the cold, black and icy water, for about a second.

Sputtering, he pushed himself back and spit out the muddy mess to breathe air again. In his panic, he had stuck his head in the water without taking a breath. Pari knew to survive he must take time to catch his breath. He needed time to take in a lung-full and then go. That is what Spike had told him to do. *I wonder if Spike is still alive.* He imagined Spike's dead body blocking his escape and was so terrified he pushed it out of his mind, pretending such a possibility did not exist. Again he found himself immobilized. The tune for Working in a Coal Mine popped back into his head, he hummed along for a minute, calming himself.

Finally a cold determination gripped him. He took a deep breath and pushed ahead into the stream without thinking. He squirmed and pushed, and he moved forward, but the tunnel went on and on. He began to run out of air and in desperation he wriggled further down the tube, but it still went down. At last he began to run out of breath. He could not open his mouth, he was still under water, to give in to the urge to breathe meant certain death. He was consumed by the desperation of suffocation. *Anything, anything for a breath*, he thought. Yet, if he gave in, death would not be instant, he knew. He opened his eyes to the murky grit and saw—nothing. Still he pushed on, and then, at the end of his ability to hold his breath, beginning to black out, he got stuck. The passage was too tight...he couldn't move. Panic topped the fear of death and he opened his mouth mindlessly. As he heard the sound of his own scream, bursting through the bubbles, consciousness began to leave him.

Then, he saw a flash of light.

Chapter 27: Chiaroscuro

Spike was still recovering from his journey through the watery tunnel when he saw mud begin to seep into the pool. He had emerged from that hole barely alive and very exhausted not five minutes before. Having made it out, he'd decided the best thing to do was to be sure this was the place where he would want Pari to follow. After the confines of the submersed rabbit hole, the 10 by 20 foot cavern felt expansive to Spike. He saw that the room led down to another, larger hole that was also flooded, but there were many good signs. The formations here were dirty—evidence that dust blew in from the outside from time to time. Also, in the upper back of the room, his light illumined a large pile of bat dung. He could see it was crawling with crickets, and they were not blind cave crickets either. When he followed the stream down to the bottom of the room, he saw an old snakeskin. Lastly, he was sure he could catch a flicker of light coming through the stream, where it exited the room.

He'd returned to the pool to sit and catch his breath. He'd seen that the water had cleared of the mud from his passage, so the murky water flowing through it now could only mean that Pari had taken the risk and decided to follow him. The pool was still clear enough to see cave pearls rocking on the bottom, and there, amid them, lay the rope he would have used to signal Pari. The rest of it's length had flowed out of the hole that supplied the pool with its water. It too rocked gently with the current.

The rocking almost lulled him to sleep, but then he noticed the flow of water stop. With a shock, he realized Pari must be stuck in the constriction that had given him the most trouble. It was just at the exit near the floor of the pool, so when he shined his light down into it, he saw Pari's grasping fingers. Then he saw a trickle of bubbles, and next, Pari's hand floated down to the silted bottom.

Spike dove into the water and swam the scant eight feet or so to the bottom in a moment. He'd left his light on at the edge, so he could see the way to Pari. Once there, he locked his hand around his wrist and began to pull, finally putting both feet on either side of the hole to get a purchase. Pari was free, pant-less, but free. On the way back to the surface, their hands clasped and he knew he had not been too late. Once he was sure Pari was stabilized, he dove back in to retrieve Pari's pants. On the way back he discovered what had been the problem, the gun had been jammed in Pari's side pocket, and it must have caught on a protuberance in the passage. By the time he returned to dry land, Pari had recovered and was grinning like an idiot.

"There are easier ways to get me to take my pants off!"

"You're in an awfully good mood for someone who just about drowned. Man, you had me freaked out!"

"Sorry, but Spike, I feel great. I feel like the whole world has been lifted from my shoulders. It just seems like everything is in perspective and what matters most is that I'm alive and I have a chance to live a conscious life."

"What are you talking about? So you were unconscious before? I don't know, maybe you're suffering from a lack of oxygen." Pari laughed.

"Not anoxia, I would know, I've treated it. No tingling, headache, numbness, dizziness, loss of vision...no, I feel quite the opposite. I feel elated and absolutely clear. Look, when I was choking, panicking and blacking out down there, I thought my life was over—dead in a rabbit hole!"

"We should call it a beaver hole." Spike grinned.

"Hmmm, I won't go there. Seriously, as I was beginning to black out, I saw a light, not the white light that you hear people talk about, but a rich, saturated, colorful light...so beautiful! Once I saw that, I realized I was not too happy with the way my life had gone untill now. Then I heard a voice. I swear it, I heard a voice saying, 'you have another chance, use it well'."

"Wow"

"Right, wow. So here's what I know, we are getting out of this and life is going to be better. I think we need to make sure whoever killed Dory comes to justice, and, between you, me and my boss we can do it....But first we have to get out."

Spike liked this new side of Pari, he found it exciting, *perhaps too exciting*, he thought, seeing Pari had noticed his body's reaction.

"Okay, give me my pants, before anything else begins to, come up." Then he began to sing, "We gotta get out of this place, if its the last thing we ever do!"

"Where did you hear that song?"

"My folks used to sing it."

"Your folks?"

"Yeah, not a typical song for Indian parents, but they are not typical. It makes me miss them too. I'm calling them when we get out."

With that, Spike led Pari down to the lower part of the cave, right up to the place where the water flowed out of the chamber. Before Spike could say a thing, Pari shouted, "Leap of faith!" and went through, without hesitating. Spike waited a moment to see if the water began to back up and then followed him down. He slid through a slick passage and popped out into the light, falling into a small pool in the middle of Beuhman's Canyon, right on top of Pari. They laughed. The light was blinding at first. Spike couldn't see a thing, but he heard Pari mutter:
"Chiaroscuro."

"What?"

"Chiaroscuro. It is an Italian term I learned in an art class at the U for extreme contrasts of light and dark. See how the morning light comes in sideways through the canyon? It highlights the cracks, and the bumps. It lights he textures of the rocks and plants in silhouette. In art, it's a way to make the important things stand out in relief. I was thinking how almost dying does the same thing."

Spike reflected on this as they walked out of the slot canyon. At first the walls were only four or five feet apart, but twenty high, then, gradually, the canyon opened to twice as wide, with drifts of boulders, gravel and sand. He wasn't as sure as Pari that the real killer would be found. He knew his friend didn't know all the details or complications around Dory and her murder. Nevertheless, he was willing to walk with this young man into a new future, illuminated by the recent past. Life looked hopeful, and it was good to feel that way. The morning light seemed to illumine everything with a special clarity, as though the world had just been made this morning. The sky was perfectly clear and the deep blue color of the ocean. The air, fresh and new, smelled like clean sheets and slaked earth. He walked next to Pari in silence: two friends, newly born, wondering at life, with the only sound being the crunch of the gravel underneath their feet.

Chapter 28: No Spark

Evy pushed the speed limit all the way across town and made it up Redington Pass in record time. She was excited to keep moving because she'd just received an alert that Pari's phone had logged in and then out. She was sure she had the approximate location, but it had been just a blip, *so it might be a bit off,* she thought. Up past Chiva falls and over the first rise she drove into a pulloff to get out her binoculars and scan the road ahead. She'd stopped because she'd seen a dust trail and hoped it might be Pari and Spike returning after a night out in the wilds. It was not the two of them. What she saw alarmed her—George Oldfather's Humvee careening down the road.

Evy watched him toss something out and saw its metallic glint in the early morning light. Whatever it was, it had lodged at the base of a large, many armed Saguaro. She decided it might be wise to lock her car up and hike a few feet off into the desert bush before he drove on by. She was sure the supervisor hadn't even noticed her vehicle as he sped down the hill.

After he was gone, Evy drove up to where he had ditched the weapon. It was an easy retrieval. *Well*, she thought, i*magine my surprise! It's a Bryco Arms 9 mm semiautomatic*. She picked it up and wrapped it in a silk scarf, protecting any fingerprints that might still be on the weapon. Then she called Officer Moreno while driving up to where she thought Pari's last signal had been. Oldfather's appearance had filled her with foreboding.

"Hey Evelyn, what's up?" For a moment she was annoyed and then decided to take Carole Anne's advice.

"Philip, what's up with me at this moment is something I've been meaning to say. I hate the name Evelyn. Every time you call me that I get pissed off."

"Is that why you called me? I mean seriously? You get pissed when I say your name?"

Evy could hear from his tone this wasn't going well. "Okay, look, I'm just asking you not to use that name. I'm not pissed off yet, just annoyed. I get this way any time anyone calls me Evelyn, but its worse when you do it—because I feel like a child when I hear you call me by that name. I want you to call me something that makes me feel good about myself."

"Well, why didn't you say so?"

Because I shouldn't have to, Stupid, she thought and instantly regretted it, but she decided a bit more truth would be good. "I wanted you to figure it out without my telling you to do it."

"I'm not a mind reader, but I guess I should have figured this out. Sorry, E... What is it you want to be called?"

"I want you to call me Evy."

"Evy! I thought that was Cory's pet name for you."

Now she knew he was pissed. *The jealousy comes out ... here we go again*, she thought. "No, Evy is not his pet name, it's my name—he just figured out—on his own. That is what I like to be called. So, do you think you could make the switch?"

"All right, Evy. I do want to make you happy. I might slip up, but I will try not to. Evy, why did you call me?"

Amazed at how much better that made her feel, she launched into where she was, what she had seen and found and what she meant to do.   "....I know this might be one of the guns you've been looking for—do you think he could be..."

"Don't jump the gun!" he laughed, "I'm on the East side now. Where are you headed? I should meet up with you, and I want you to show me exactly where you found it."

"I've got to go find Pari."

"No, you don't. This is now police business. Wait for me. I need to see where you found the gun. Also, I don't want you to go alone in case..."

"In case there's been another murder?"

"Exactly, I'll be there in fifteen minutes or less. Meanwhile, please don't call—Oh hell, forget it, I know you'll tell him anyway, call Cory, but when you do, ask him to keep it quiet. If Oldfather is involved I have to have a very tight case or he'll slip through my fingers before I start to grab."

Of course, the moment Philip hung up, Evy was on the phone to Cory.

☼

Carole Anne loved the feel of clean air on her skin. A breeze was good, but the wind from a cycle ride pushing her hair back was the best. This morning the air was brisk but not too cold, perfect. She also loved this ride around Mount Lemmon...the Lemmon. That was how she'd always thought of it. She enjoyed skiing and Mt. Lemmon, the highest peak in the Catalinas, had the southernmost ski area in the nation.

She'd made the way through town without hitting a single stoplight. It was as though the Universe had opened all its gates. She flew through Oro Valley, past magnificent Pusch Ridge, through the town of Catalina and all the way to Oracle in what seemed like minutes. She was in rare form, pushing her bike as fast as it would go. The dirt road encircling the north side of mountains had been recently graded and made a perfect surface for her run. Twice she nearly collided with vehicles coming the opposite way around tight bends, but the close calls just filled her with exhilaration. What was almost unbearable was the dust streaming out behind the passing cars. Both times she felt the engine cough and sputter with the fine dust, but each time it caught and she went on.

Highway 76 split at the San Pedro River, and she took Redington Road to the South. Twice she took dips through washes that ran down from the Catalina Mountains just a bit too fast. Though she loved that roller-coaster feeling, fishtailing the dirt road after coming back down was not wise.

After the second jump, she slowed down and the engine coughed again. *Troubling*. She slowed down and tried to remember what tools she had. That was when she saw Woody's truck barreling toward her. *Small world and sticky,* she thought, feeling for a moment again the awful sense of claustrophobia she'd set out on this journey to escape. Her first thought was to gun it past him and hope he wouldn't recognize her, but when she applied the throttle, the engine died. She decided there was nothing to do but bluff it out and did her best to make it look like she was pulling over and parking the bike on purpose. Woody caught sight of her and braked to a stop. She'd dismounted and stood, arms crossed, unflinching while the dust swirled around her. Woody got out of his truck and grinned. It sparked old feelings in a moment, despite her wish that it wouldn't. She stood looking at him for more than a minute, unflinching, Woody broke first.

"Girl, you are looking fine. Delicioso!"

"Cut the crap, Woody. What the hell are you doing out here?" Carole Anne believed in offense as defense.

"Oh, just visiting old playgrounds. What about you, my sexy mama?"

"Never you mind. By the way, I think you owe me some rent."

He laughed. "You have more cojones than any of the guys that work for me. I don't think so, Baby! Unless that little Chiquita gave you back the deed before she died."

Shit, how much does he know? "The Deed went back to me at her death," she said, hoping her bluff would work.

"To you? Why? What are you, her mother?" He said this with his best attempt at sarcasm, but she saw him catch the change in her face.   "Son of a bitch, you are her mother! Estupido!"

She laughed out loud when he hit himself in the head. Sometimes he telegraphed every thought. She couldn't resist enjoying his slow recognition of what had escaped him for so long. However, she wanted to get out of there before anything else came to his mind—such as who the father might be. She wasn't ready for that conversation, so she kept up the bluff to keep him on her track.

"Yeah, so you owe me rent. By the way, those people can buy your house, but they still have to negotiate with me to live in it...or, you can do it directly. I think you should split half of what you make with me, just to clear the title. Then I'll go away." He was still rubbing his head and speaking to the air. He showed no sign of hearing anything she'd just said.

"Claro. So, that is why Deels pushed me out...cabron!"

She could see that he clearly thought Dory was Deel's daughter. He turned to her,

"Caroleena, are you going to Deel's cena, to that asshole's dinner party?"

She was a little shocked, she'd not known Woody had been on the guest list. Her answer flew from her lips. "Yes." When Woody grinned, she used to think the grimace would scare children. It still scared her. *Schadenfreude* she thought, she knew he often took deep pleasure in the misfortune of others and wondered what ill tidings he was imagining...*and if he takes pleasure in the pain of others and I know it, why am I drawn to him?* She wondered.

He broke from his revery and spoke to her. "Then I will see you later, mi esposa una vez."

With that he hopped back in his truck and set off down the road. The reference shocked her. She had said those very words to him not long ago. She thought back to the last time they had met, the last time they'd had words, on the day Dory had died. Woody had caught her sneaking around Scorpion Path, on the hill just outside his bedroom. There had been no flirting that day—he was pissed. He'd thought she'd been there to spy on him she supposed, or worse. He'd accused her of fucking up his life and demanded to know way she'd given her Estate for Life to Dory.

She couldn't come clean with him then. Guilty at withholding his daughter from him, guilty from losing her relationship with Dory, afraid that Dory was in a mess she couldn't help her out of and, finally, being caught red-handed spying on his house, she'd attacked him. She'd thrown every insult and injury she could think of his way. When his rage erupted she drew her gun and told him calmly that she'd come out to the desert to shoot snakes. "If you get in the way, that's too bad...mi esposa una vez." Things would have escalated further, but at that moment they heard a car drive up and someone get out. They were on the opposite side of the building, so she couldn't see who it was, but obviously Woody knew. He shouted out a curse and turned to look at the house.

"Pinche cabron! That fucking agent is back..." He turned to Carole Anne and, with a swipe of his hammy fist, knocked the gun aside. It went off and flew from her hand to land in an ocotillo a few feet away. She'd turned to see a part of the glass ceiling breaking. "Shit!" he said, "Largarse, get out of here, I have more important things to do than fuck with you."

She remembered a series of things happening next in what seemed like an instant. The wind shifted and a dust devil swirled down the hill bringing with it an unpleasant smell...the scent of sour sweat and Old Spice. An alarm began to shriek. Woody ran down the hill toward the house. Carole Anne grabbed her gun out of the ocotillo. While picking it up she saw someone on the hillside above. She couldn't tell who it was, but he was sighting a gun toward the house. She glanced back toward the house. There, she could see, through the now open atrium ceiling, her daughter shaking her fist at someone. She looked back and shouted at the person up the hill. He turned the gun sight at her and fired. Dirt sprayed her as the bullet hit. She began to run, immediately tripping on a cat claw vine. She was trying to see who was coming down the hill, still aiming at her, but with little success as the dust had blinded her. Another shot made the dirt explode near her foot. She aimed her gun at the man up the hill. Dolores Samaniego appeared, running up the hill toward her. *Were did she come from?* Carole Anne thought, but had no idea. She saw the man aim back at her daughter; she thought she had to stop him.

Just then, Dolores grabbed her hand and pulled, shouting "No! Don't shoot, Carole Anne!" The moment seemed as if she were in a dream, then and now. Dolores had that bland, pleasant expression that meant trouble. They fought over the gun, pulling it back and forth. Then, as Dolores jerked her hand a last time, Caole Anne's gun and the man's both went off. She fell down, dropped the gun and saw the man up above began to pick his way down the hill toward them. Two more shots came from inside the house. She got up and ran from this madness. As she did, she glanced back at Dolores who'd grabbed the gun and was running up the hill towards the shooting man. As she ran, Caole Anne looked back at the house, but she could no longer see her daughter. She fled, found her bike, and was out of that scene of chaos in moments. Later, she and Dolores would have words that ended their friendship. Later, when she found out her daughter had been murdered.

She shook herself out of this revery and turned the key again. No spark.

Chapter 29: Happiness is a Warm Gun

Officer Moreno examined the camping site near the cave-in covering Spike's jeep. The slide had covered all trace of the vehicle, but the tracks led right up to the pile of dirt. No genius was necessary to see what had happened here. Last night's campers had also left the place a mess. Despite his training, he was tempted to clean it. Instead, he documented what he saw and collected evidence. He assumed Pari's phone had winked out right here, shortly after the cave-in, through a loss of signal.

It had been child's play for him to find this place from the coordinates Evy gave him, but he hadn't really needed them. The chase the previous day had left a path more obvious than a buffalo stampede—from the staging area entrance on. He was glad Evy had given him the coordinates, but also happy she wasn't with him now. He loved her, but when she was around, his work suffered.

Cory had demanded she return to work after she had called in, apparently to help him prepare for his dinner party. Cory had called Moreno directly thereafter to ask if he would share news about the young men, should he find them. Moreno suggested a tit for tat and Cory volunteered the guest list for the evening, plus a few of his suppositions. When that didn't produce the desired results he also mentioned that Carole Anne Michaels was on her way around the Catalinas from Oracle. That trade was good enough for Moreno. Carole Anne was still on his list.

Philip Moreno kept an evidence kit in his unmarked SUV. It took an hour to catalog the scene—spent casings, MRE leftovers and drink cans all went in bags; he cast foot prints and tire tracks, took photos. Then he called the site in to the sheriff's office, so others could dig out the jeep—he wasn't equipped to do that. He knew this cave led down to Beuhman's Canyon, it was common knowledge in the county rescue community. Beuhman's was where Evy had picked up the second signal, so he wasn't too worried there might be bodies there, but he was a little concerned about Carole Anne. It was evident to him that there'd been two vehicles and two men in the arroyo. He supposed the other party had traveled back toward Oracle, so there was a good chance he and Carole Anne would cross paths. He examined the tracks of the truck higher up the hill. There were good imprints here from the Humvee and the other truck. The ground had a bit of a seep so the slightly boggy earth cast as good an image as plaster could take. The truck's tires had a distinctive tread. He knew them well: Nitto Terra Grapplers, popular with off-roaders, but expensive enough to be relatively rare.

He drove on out, following the road down to the turnoff. One way went to Benson, the other to Oracle. He immediately spotted the heavy duty treads heading off in the direction to Beuhman's and knew the driver had taken the road to Oracle. He stepped on it, and turned the CD player back on. The Beatles White Album had picked up at "Glass Onion" and he sang along for the next few songs. Finally he came to the road leading up to Beuhman's. Lennon was singing "She's not a girl who misses much" when he spotted Carole Anne up ahead, pulled off of the side of the road working on her motorcycle. "Oh yeah," he sang along as he drove up to her, "She's well acquainted with the touch of a velvet hand..."

She didn't pay any attention to him as he slowed down. This was a familiar scenario. Moreno had found that when people are guilty they pretend as though they don't even see him, but he knew she knew he was there. As he stepped out of his SUV, she raised an eye and looked back at what she was doing—re-seating a spark plug, he thought. "Hi Carole Anne, need help?"

"Nope, just about got it fixed, but thanks, Philip."

She amazed him with her cooler than thou attitude. Most people would shake a little at such a chance meeting. "Well, that's good. Look, I'm up here looking for the same two you are. I don't suppose you passed anyone on the way?"

"If you mean Spike Smith or Pari Workingboxwalla, no."

"Nope, I'm thinking of a tall, heavy guy driving a four-wheel truck." He saw she knew who it was, and he supposed she knew she'd given it away.

"Yeah, I saw him. Woody Madrone. He just passed me on the way back to town through Oracle."

"Busy day on the backside of the mountain."

She laughed. "You can say that again. You looking for him too?"

"Not necessarily, but I could be in the future."

Just then he saw Carole Anne's eyes widen. He turned to see Spike and Pari making their way out of the canyon. Pari was grinning broadly and began to wave and shout and run in their direction. Spike seemed less enthusiastic. *Perhaps he wasn't so happy about was who was doing the rescuing,* Philip thought. He'd had run-ins with both young men in the past, but his encounters with Spike had been a bit more serious. He turned to Carole Anne and finished their conversation.

"Look, Carole Anne. You're not my prime suspect here, but I know you haven't told me everything. I'm not a fool, and I know you were at Scorpion Path the day Dory died." Her eyebrows raised.

"Tire-tracks, my specialty. I am asking you now: Will you be at Cory's this evening? I want to hear a yes. Otherwise, we might have to leave your bike here."

He knew Carole Anne. Normally she would have come back with a jibe, but not this time. She smiled, stowed the repair kit, turned the key and kicked the bike awake. The motor hummed.

She popped up the kick stand while she spoke: "I'll be there Officer Moreno."

He watched her speed by Pari and Spike. The wind caught her dust trail and for a moment he couldn't see any of them. Then the air cleared as she topped the hill and was gone. He picked the guys up and gave them some water and a couple of protein bars that he kept stashed in the glove box for emergencies. They were in remarkably good condition for the adventure they'd been through, and clean, since they'd washed off in Beuhman's creek when they'd come out of the cave. The walk had dried them out and they looked no worse than any campers. Moreno noticed the bulge in Pari's cargo pocket and asked about it. When he produced the gun, Philip's heart stopped for a moment. It was a Ruger SR9c Compact Pistol, the missing gun from the crime scene.
"Where did this pistol come from, guys?" Spike looked up.

"I picked it up at the All Soul's Procession."

"Come again?" Spike told the good officer all the events that had led up to its acquisition.

"Interesting. You won't mind if I keep it will you? After all, you don't have a permit."

Both of them seemed relieved to be rid of it. He called in to the station and then also let Evy and Cory know that he had picked up the guys and expected to have them back in town by noon. As they made their way down Redington Pass, he popped the CD back in. John Lennon picked up where he had left off, and Philip Moreno laughed as he sang the final words to the song: "Well...don't you know that happiness is a warm gun."

Chapter 30: Them That's Got, Shall Get

The house was buzzing when Pari arrived with Spike. Officer Moreno had dropped them off in the parking lot behind the house, saying he was going straight to the station. Pari suspected he would check the ballistics of the gun before dinner, though he didn't mention that. He could see through the glass that Evelyn had closed up the front desk and installed Harry Wu in the conference room. Pari suggested Spike just stay at the house with him rather than going home and coming back. Besides, he was famished and was sure Spike could use a meal too. They entered through the garage door into chaos.

Cory was in the midst of final prep when he saw them, and he looked ready to explode. He took one look at Pari and then turned away as he shouted: "You two are filthy! Get out of my kitchen."

Pari thought he was joking and asked if he had anything they could eat for lunch.

Cory slowly turned to them, looking as mad as a bee in a shook bottle. "Get out, confound it. Go find yourself something in the game room kitchen—but wash first!"

They left in a hurry. Pari led Spike to his rooms and they took turns showering. Spike suggested they shower together, but Pari really wasn't ready to take the next step in any relationship. When he told Spike that, he could see that his friend was crestfallen. Pari gave him a hug and told him when they took that step he wanted it to mean something. That seemed to help. He slapped Spike on the butt and sent him to shower.

Pari was in a pensive mood. *There's been altogether too much dying recently not to start thinking things through.* His recent brushes with death had helped him realize that he'd been given an opportunity to live more deeply. He looked on these events as fortuitous, not just chance. *I can either live life unconsciously, as I always have*, he thought, *or begin to reassess what I do and live with my eyes open.* He desperately wanted to retain this new feeling of being fully awake.

He lent Spike some clothes and they fit—he thought it was great to see Spike in colors other than black. After Pari had showered they ate lunch in the game room: Smoked Salmon, Cory's cured olives, rusk, baba ganush, dried apricots. Pari was used to this fare by now but Spike just poked at it. *I'm sure he's wishing for a hamburger,* Pari thought.

Evy burst into the room, surprising them. To Pari, she looked like a kid who knew there would be no dessert till after she ate the broccoli.

She wrinkled her nose at Spike, speaking directly to Pari. "Cory has some special instructions for you. He asked me to tell you to visit him in his quarters in five minutes." She turned to Spike, "You may stay here until the dinner. Be aware; there are security cameras everywhere. Your every move will be watched."

With that Evelyn walked out of the room. Pari was appalled but Spike didn't seem to be put off at all. In stead, he laughed when he saw Pari's expression. "You get used to this kind of treatment when you wear the clothes I wear." Then he looked down and laughed again, "Oh, right, I'm not wearing those clothes."

Pari knew the feeling of being unjustly judged. He was embarrassed but he could also see that Evy was just trying to protect him. On his way into Cory's room he tried to soften Evy's warnings,   "Spike, you're free to go where you wish in the house, and you can stay here, or in my rooms, either one."

"I'm fine right here, don't worry!"

Pari had been in Cory's sanctum only a couple of times, but it didn't get old. Cory loved music, so he'd had the room absolutely soundproofed. Pari opened the door from silence to a flood of music, the volume was shocking and overwhelming. He recognized the piece from some movie or another he'd seen. Kettle drums boomed, and snares banged, reminding him of the gunshots he'd heard the day Dory died. Then a chorus of women wailed from high to low echoing a scream. Cory motioned him to sit. The piece was over in a few minutes, but Cory sat still, a hand on his forehead, deep in thought. Pari didn't understand why the music affected him so deeply, but again he was plunged into remorse. Finally Cory looked up at the him and spoke.

"That was 'Dies Irae' from The Messa da Requiem by Giuseppe Verdi. It was conducted by Zubin Mehta. He's a Parsi, like you."

Pari liked that, *Parsi's are a rare breed,* he thought.

"The words you came in on mean, This day of adjudication will dissolve the World into ashes, everything will be strictly evaluated!"

"Am I being judged?" Pari asked, but Cory just chuckled.

"No, my boy, not at all. As near as I can tell, you are nearly blameless. Your friend, however, may be more involved."

"Spike?" *Why would he be involved—how could he have been?* Pari had thought many times about who might have killed Dory, but all he really knew was that he wasn't the one. The idea that Spike could be involved seemed absurd. He heard Cory's voice, but he was speaking to himself.

"Your instincts are right, we must be careful in our judging, lest we be judged and found wanting."

Pari found this train of thought bewildering and decided to try to cut through to what was important. "I had a very intense experience yesterday, Cory. I thought I was dying. I thought there was no hope, but when I made it out everything felt different. The world was fresh and new—it still feels that way to me."

"These are normal feelings for such a close call."

"Okay, but my point is that it woke me up. I felt then and I still do now that I need to judge myself. When I take a good look at me, I know I have to change direction."

Cory looked skeptical. "What is your plan for change? People seldom make any real changes."

"I'll start by thanking you, today, now—for everything you've done for me."

Cory laughed. "Pari, I appreciate it. You are welcome and I thank you." He laughed again.

"I'm serious."

"Don't get too serious. You would lose your charm."

Pari finished filling Cory in on everything that had happened. It seemed to him that Cory found little surprising, except the gun. After that came up, Cory questioned him in detail, and Pari told him exactly how Spike said he had come by the weapon. Then Cory explained Pari's part in the rest of the evening.

"I want you to understand," Cory said, "normally I would not get involved in police business, but we have a contract to fulfill with our clients, the Brooks. The police are moving at glacial speed, and that is not good enough. To secure this house for Rupert and Dana, the title must be clear of clouds. Unfortunately the Estate for Life I once gave to Carole Anne, and that she then gave to her daughter— further complicated by Dory's death—has created a huge cloud on the title. If the death had been natural or if we knew where the Estate for Life was it might be different, but that is not the case. As a result, I have decided that this evening we will have a play in three acts. I believe the answer to all these questions will be revealed in our drama."

"A play?"

"Yes, except most of the main actors will not realize they are playing roles in our script. It is imperative that neither you nor Spike can be seen in the first act, though you will still play a part." Pari was puzzled, but Cory clarified. "We need Woody Madrone and George Oldfather to believe you were both lost in that cave, at least at the beginning. You two will dress as members of the party staff, all of whom will wear costumes and masks."

"The staff?" Before this, a dinner party to Pari meant either a pizza and a six pack at his house, or rice and chicken tikka with a visiting professor or relative at his folks place. A staff, masks and costumes seemed over the top to him.

"My dinners are well known. I always have a theme, entertainment and a staff. I do not have dinner parties so I can slave in the kitchen and at the bar. My dinners are for my pleasure as well as the pleasure of others. Sometimes I have another agenda, as tonight, but creating a rich experience is always first. I bring people together so I can meet them and we can enjoy each other's company. So, yes, we have a staff. I've hired Johnny West as bartender and Billy Jo Zane as DJ and back-up for the singer. I had also hired a few others to serve, but now you and Spike will take these roles."

Pari was fascinated and amazed. "You have a singer for tonight?"

"Almeta Speaks is in town, she's an old friend. She's agreed to sing a few numbers for the cocktail hour. Evy will be helping you serve. Remember, you will all be in costume. I have a half dozen shills coming in to fill out the party-goers."

"Shills?"

"People in the crowd, usually paid, who are in on the con, so to speak. I want enough folks at the beginning to keep the main players from cutting each other's throats until just the right time. I have styled this dinner as a wake, a remembrance of the dead, specifically a wake for Dory and Mary. I will want you to listen carefully, pay attention to who gathers together and what is said."

"What kind of costume and masks?" Pari asked.

"Skulls—skulls and black cowls. You two will remain in costume until the dinner itself."

Pari was given a few more instructions, including who to listen to and how, and when to join the "second act." Then Cory told him to summon Spike. Cory wanted to give him instructions in person.

After Cory was finished with Spike, Pari showed him the rest of the house and the Brokerage. The dining and drawing rooms had been set up for the party, but the drawing room was the real surprise —it looked as though Cory was expecting more like thirty than eleven. Billy Jo Zane was already there and had set up a DJ booth and a little stage opposite the French doors leading to the Courtyard, Johnny West was in the house too, setting up the bar. Pari knew both of them moonlighted as security and bodyguard, but these roles were new to him. Almeta Speaks, the jazz singer, was already warming up. She wore the cowl, but not the mask which would have prevented her from singing. Cory had told him the short program he had scheduled: "Strange Fruit," "Pretty Polly," "St. James infirmary," and "God Bless the Child." Pari thought it was a very dark mix, but no one could accuse Cory of holding back.

Pari and Spike left to put on their costumes. When they returned, the rest of the staff were already wearing theirs, waiting for the guests to arrive. They looked like a cult—members of an underworld monastery. Pari knew everyone had received the same basic instructions—to remain silent and use gestures to communicate. When guests arrived, they were to be made to wait at the entrance of the Passadizo until one of the "monks" opened the gate and allowed them inside, one by one, guiding each to a massive table set up against the back gate. It was a kind of altar de muertos, an altar of the dead.

Pari and Spike had earlier hung pictures of the Samaniego girls in black and white on the gate. On either side of these pictures they had placed tall vases of black Calla lilies and laid a spray of white roses on the table underneath each picture, with one black rose on top of each bunch, laid in the opposite direction. Forty-one pillar candles, representing the combined ages of Mary and Dory, lit the table. All were white except the two under each picture, these two were black. Black silk scarves flowed out of a bowl in the center behind a registration book. Pari and Spike, the "monks" led each guest to the table in silence and tied a black silk scarf around the arm of each one while they signed their names and wrote their condolences. Then, one by one they led the guests into the drawing room.

The lights there were dimmed from their normal brilliance, which only increased the feeling of size and depth. The logs in the fireplace had been replaced with two unlit torches flanked on either side by 41 lighted candles and two tall vases of black callas...reminding everyone of the Altar of the dead out in the pasadizo.

All went well, with the shills following this routine and the real guests following them until George Oldfather arrived. He began to make a stink about signing the register and refused to wear the armband. Pari motioned the largest monk over to assist. Johnny West physically held Oldfather down and tied on the band. Johnny held him there without speaking until the Supervisor signed. West then brought him into the drawing room and poured him a 151 rum and coke. That seemed to satisfy him. When Pari's clients arrived, they just followed suit but Pari could see that they were thrown by the affair.

Once the rest of the guests entered the drawing room, Pari and Spike gave each one a garland of marigolds to wear and a cocktail, then left then to wander. The marigolds were a nod to Mexican death customs, but the garlands reminded Pari of his parents' home and his trip to India. He felt a stab of regret and again silently vowed to call them and repair the rift. Spike and Pari circulated with canapés. The guests mingled in the room, hung out by the art and chatted in low tones. Thus far the party was very low key and Pari thought nothing much seemed to be happening.

The singer, Almeta Speaks, had been accompanying herself on the piano. She had such a rich, mellow tone, Pari kept stopping to listen, entranced by her voice. She had a way of making each phrase personal. He felt she was singing to him alone about events the two of them shared. If Cory hadn't told Pari about the selected songs, he wouldn't have known each had to do with greed, death and dying, but even without his knowing the words, her voice let him know they were about suffering and the human condition. He found it strange that others could ignore her performance; drinking, laughing and talking over this gift.

When he turned his attention back to the party he saw that Woody Madrone had arrived just after Supervisor Oldfather and though they pointedly avoided each other, it was clear to Pari both were nervous and taking cues from each other.

Pari kept a close eye on his clients as they talked to Ms. Speaks, and then to Philip Moreno who had walked in just after

Madrone and Oldfather arrived. He was not in uniform, but his plain clothes didn't do much to hide his profession. Pari thought police often seem to look as though they're still wearing bulletproof vests, even when in street clothes.

By this time Evelyn had taken her robes off and had joined the gathering as a member of the party. On cue, she brought Philip and Pari's clients into a gathering of shills near the fireplace just about the time Dolores Samaniego made her entrance. Dolores chatted with Woody for a few minutes then made her way past Oldfather just as Pari was delivering a plate of skewered shrimp. Oldfather mumbled something to her and Pari overheard her replying, "You had better be very careful tonight, George, Cory has wind of what you've been up too."

"I don't know what you're talking about," he hissed at her.

Pari knew Cory had persuaded Carole Anne to show up at the last minute, just before the party was to move to the dining room. When she arrived, he saw her glance at Woody, then turn away, only to see George Oldfather. Her reaction was so visceral it seemed to Pari she might stab him with a shrimp skewer. Then Cory walked in. He had dressed in one of the cowls, but he wore no mask. His robes had quite the opposite effect on his body than the costumes did on the staff. They all blended perfectly, and the robes hid their bodies in a mass of sackcloth, but on Cory the material looked rich and sensual, not monastic. The folds of cloth accentuated his physique and draped from his shoulders like the cape on a Greek statue. The hood dropped from his head as if placed there to frame his golden curls and chiseled features. He was magnetic and powerful in a way Pari had not seen before. *It must be because he's in his element...entertaining in his house, carrying out his plan, his everything.*

The room turned to him and he laughed, just as Almeta Speaks finished the last chorus of "God Bless the Child." Pari thought Cory certainly "had his own" and showed it. He circulated throughout the room greeting each person by name and having brief conversations with everyone. Some seemed cold at first but his charm seemed to put everyone at ease and soon the party was really beginning to come together. Then he hit a small gong kept on the mantle of the fireplace. The room dropped to silence.

"Thank you. Thank you all for coming. All our expected guests have arrived but two, and we shall not wait for them." Woody shuffled and George Oldfather strained to look indifferent. "You have been called here for a reason. We are gathered to celebrate life, as we remember those who have left it. Two young, beautiful women like roses in full bloom, have been cut at the very moment their petals unfurled." He pulled two long stemmed black roses off of the mantle where they had lain unnoticed until now and held them aloft. "Now I say to you that tonight we will eulogize and remember these young women as they should be celebrated!"

With that he turned to the fireplace and thrust the roses into the candle flames. They both exploded in fire. Pari had no idea what trick he had played, what solvent or magic might be responsible, but it appeared to him that the roses shown in those flames like living things, vibrant and untouched by the blue and yellow tongues of light, and yet he could feel the heat from them. *Heat that somehow does not wilt the bloom!* Pari thought. Cory spun around to the crowd and the image was so starling everyone gasped as one. He held the burning roses high in his left hand and raised them higher still. In his right he produced a drink and raised it as well. "I toast, let us all toast to the brief life of the Samaniego sisters, to the bright fire of youth extinguished, and to you—their friends and enemies, present and absent—let us toast to you as well! Salud, to Mary!" The shills in the audience shouted "Salud to Mary!" right after him and all drank from their glasses.

Cory raised his glass again and shouted "Salud, to Dory!" and drank again from his glass. Again the company followed suit, though all spoke the toast this time. Then he turned to the fireplace, lit the two torches with the roses, and dropped them down on the hearth where they sputtered and died. Next, he threw his glass into the fireplace. The sound of it shattering behind the torches brought the room to silence, except for George Oldfather who giggled. His giggles were silenced by a slap across the face from Dolores Samaniego. Pari was astonished by his boss's showmanship.

Cory spoke again. "Dinner will be served for those that have a stomach to eat and the will to stay for their desserts."

He pulled on a hidden lever in the fireplace surround and the bookcase between the drawing room and the dining room pivoted to the side leaving an opening for the guests and staff to enter.

Pari and Spike followed him through the doors and into the kitchen while the rest of the cowled staff began to move the guests forward to the dining room.

Chapter 31: Hasta los Huesos

A few moments later Pari looked through the spy hole in the swinging kitchen door and watched the guests filter in from the drawing to the dining room. The passage created by the swinging bookcase made a broad avenue which looked permanent when open. He could see that the shills Cory had invited had skillfully filtered themselves out of the mix one by one until only the invitees were left in the room. Officer Moreno deftly closed the pivoting bookcase that joined the two rooms. It moved silently on its hinge and closed largely unnoticed ... even the clack of the latch passed without comment.

Carole Anne, who had been talking to Woody, led him over to their adjoining seats. Dolores was speaking in hushed tones to George Oldfather, who seemed to have forgiven her for the slap. She steered him to his place on the other side of Carole Anne. Pari watched Dolores turn to Carole Anne and motion that they switch seats. He assumed it was so she could continue their conversation. Carole Anne happily obliged, visibly relieved to move across the table from the Supervisor, rather than sit next to him. Cory glowered at Dolores's switch in seating, but except the hint of a smile, she ignored him.

Evy and Philip took Rupert and Dana in hand, and when they were at their places Cory picked up a spoon and tapped on his glass, silencing the commotion. Even in the kitchen, peering through the spy hole, Pari found the sound arresting. The high pitched clink of silver on crystal seemed hopelessly antiquated, yet it commanded instant silence and attention. He realized at that moment that the power of an action lies in the actor, not the action itself. When a person has authority and behaves authentically, he commands attention. The maestro spoke:

"Thank you for coming to this dinner. We are here to honor the memory of Dory and Mary Samaniego, whose brief and unfortunate lives were cut short before they had any chance to find themselves." The room was deathly silent for a moment.

Then Pari and Spike walked into the dining room, still wearing their masks and cowls and began to serve the soup. Cory looked up and said, "Unfortunate that my agent Pari Workingboxwalla and his friend Spike Smith have not yet joined our dinner party, but it is late and we must proceed." Pari placed the first bowl in front of Dolores and the second in front of Woody. Spike served Carole Anne and Oldfather, while Johnny and Billy served the Brooks and the rest of the table. Spike and Pari took up positions on either side of the table. Evy ostentatiously looked at her phone and bent over to whisper to Cory.

He looked pleased. "I understand Pari and Spike are on their way and will join us later in the evening."

Madrone and Oldfather looked at each other and both began to get up.

Cory smiled, "Gentlemen, is there anything you need?"

Woody looked at George and said, "Siéntense! Our host has given us everything we need, no?" and now he turned back to Cory, "Amigo, conoces ... you know Supervisor Oldfather and I are busy men, so we hope that you will excuse us immediately after your dinner. I am glad you have brought this group together because once this wonderful young couple have purchased my home, I will be leaving town, and there are so many here I wish to say goodbye to, not the least of whom is you, Señor Deels."

Cory smiled at him. "If it is in my power, you shall have the chance. But first we will have our small celebration."

Dolores took the hand of Woody Madrone and then George Oldfather and gently seated each with a smile at Cory. Johnny West and Billy Jo Zane locked the French doors leading out of the room. Philip Moreno left his station by the revolving bookcase and took his seat. Every exit had been closed except the one to the kitchen, Johnny West and Billy Jo effectively guarded that door after serving the rest of the table. It was clear to Pari that no one would leave easily.

"So," Cory stood, "to continue my toast: To the Samaniego girls!" All raised a glass, but it was obvious that many raised theirs reluctantly. Cory continued, "You all should raise a glass with gusto. Everyone in this room had a tie with them. Some profited and some experienced loss from them, but everyone in this room is complicit in their deaths." *People might have been uncomfortable before but I bet everyone is nervous now,* Pari thought. The Brooks, Pari's clients, really stirred. Rupert began to speak but Cory cut him off. "Yes sir, even you."

Rupert stood. "I don't think so. I am not sure what game you are playing, but I am not willing to go along. My wife and I will forego your dinner. Thanks for the invitation, but we'll return when our agent is here to accompany us."

"I am your agent, sir. Please sit. Perhaps, Pari, who is my agent, did not fully explain the principle. He works for me, while I work for you. In reality, you hired me when you signed with him. Your relationship is with me alone, as far as this transaction goes. I am your fiduciary agent, so I am bound to act in your interests primarily, and not my own. You can trust me when I say that everything I do tonight will benefit you. You must stay."

"Even if I accept that, we never met Mary, and we barely knew Dory. How can you say Dana and I are somehow connected with their deaths?"

Spike stirred and Pari felt very uncomfortable. *These are my friends and clients*, he thought. He could not understand what Cory was doing. Then he saw Dana kick Rupert under the table, and realized there must be more to their story than he knew. He thought Cory was gong to speak again, but Dolores spoke instead.

"I raised these girls, they were my daughters, and Mary told me what was going on in her life. I knew the first time she used. It was with Spike Smith. I believe you know him?"

Rupert visibly paled, "Yes, but."

"But nothing young man. Mary said they were stopping off at University Hospital one night, the night she first tried drugs, to drop off some cocaine to a couple of the interns." Spike coughed, but no one else seemed to notice.

"What are you implying?" Rupert looked defiant but Pari could see Dana shrinking in her seat.

Officer Moreno laughed. "Everyone in the department knows you interns buy drugs. We followed Spike to keep track of the smalltime users who bought through him, though he didn't know it. Sorry Rupert. We were aware of your habits, but we were looking for bigger fish." He glanced at Oldfather, who pointedly ignored him,

Dolores spoke again to Moreno. "Do you know who got the drugs that night?" Spike shifted uncomfortably while officer Moreno spoke.

"Rupert called him on his cell regularly, I know, I've pulled his records. If it wasn't that night, it was another."

"No," Dolores said, "I questioned Mary after she came home so late that first night. She said the drugs were for a friend of Spike's and that his friend was celebrating his marriage to another intern."

Dana looked very upset. "That was us."

Rupert looked at her and stood up again so rapidly he knocked his chair back, Dana grabbed it and pushed it back in place and pulled him down while she spoke. "The less you say right now, the better, my husband."

He sat down and picked up his soup spoon, muttering, "She's right, that was us."

Cory looked satisfied and spoke again. "Yes, each of us knows a piece of this puzzle, because each of us is involved, but now, it is time for soup. This is levanta muertos a catchall dish, much like our dinner party, popular from Peru to the Dominican Republic, where this recipe originates. The name means "raise the dead," and so we shall."

Everyone began to eat, but Pari could see Oldfather was still looking for a way out. The supervisor put his spoon down as if to speak when Dolores Samaniego cut him off.

"I have a bit more to say on this subject. After all, these were my girls."

Carole Anne looked up from her bowl, set her spoon down and stood, "I've had enough of that, They were not "your girls," Mary was yours; Dory was my daughter!"

Dolores looked coolly over the table at her. "You forfeited that title when you abandoned her." She picked up her water and sipped.

"You bitch."

Woody turned to Dolores. "Good of you to take their kid in like you did."

In her rage, Carole Anne turned on him. "Shut up. Couldn't you tell? Didn't you know? Dory tried to tell you but you kept pushing her away."

"¿Qué?"

"She was your daughter, Woody."

His face drained of blood and he pushed his bowl back and mumbled. "Madre de Dios. I thought she was just saying those things to me to get me to do what she wanted. Estupido, Dios mio."

Oldfather began to snicker again but halted immediately when Dolores raised her hand. Cory motioned for the bowls to be taken away,

Carole Anne wasn't finished, though.

She turned to Dolores. "You're right, Woody, it was good of them to take our child. I thought I was doing the right thing for her— giving her a real home, but I should have kept her with me. At least she would have had a mother with visible feelings instead of this cold woman with the face of an ice-cube."

Mrs. Samaniego refused to be moved by this attack. She only smiled back.

Carole Anne continued to goad her, "I thought being an orphan yourself, you would have given her the love you lacked. But you withheld it from Dory while showering all of it on Mary."

"Shut up." Dolores hardly raised her voice but the quiet words hit the room like a scream.

"Why? You deserve to hear this, Dory was lucky to have a crust of bread in your home."

Pari was amazed at the fireworks going on in the room and wondered if Carole Anne had listened to the words of "God Bless the Child," and pulled the words crust of bread from it on purpose. *Whatever the case, it seems to have hit the mark,* he thought.

Dolores smiled again, took another sip of her water, and tossed the rest in Carole Anne's face. Carole Anne must have just taken a breath, because she began to choke and sputter. She finally sat down, trying to recover. Officer Moreno wiped the water from her brow and tried to comfort her, but she pushed his hand away. Before anyone else had a chance to speak, Dolores took the gavel.

"You are correct, though...I did not love them in the same way. What parent can say their love is given equally? So you see, I did love Dory. We were close, before her sister died. After that, I couldn't reach her, and the distance only got worse once you showed up to try to reclaim her. Why did you do that? What gave you the right to tell her you were her mother after so many years?" The tension in the room grew. No one spoke for a moment. "I wouldn't have told you this," Dolores said with a sad look, "but it was me she called on in that final day, not you."

Carole Anne looked up, finally. "She called me too. That's why I came."

Cory spoke up, "Dory was a busy girl that morning. She called many of you who are present, isn't that true, Officer?"

Moreno spoke, "Yes, I pulled her cell phone records. She did call you, Carole Anne—but also Dolores, Spike, Pari, our esteemed Supervisor, and you Woody—even Rupert Brooks."

Rupert looked up again, Dana appeared shocked. "I didn't answer," he told her quickly.

"No, not that time, but you two had conversations earlier in the week."

Dana looked fit to be tied, "Why didn't you tell me this?"

Rupert looked away as he spoke. "I knew she had the deed, I'd heard it from Spike, and I was trying to work things out."

Dana looked more than a little pissed. The room got quiet again.

Finally Supervisor Oldfather pushed his chair up and stood. "I agree with Rupert. I'm not sure what kind of game is being played here, but I have no interest in it, or in all of you grieving idiots. Thanks for the soup, I'll forgo the nuts."

Cory raised an eyebrow and motioned for Spike and me to block either side of the table. "I think not. We haven't begun to talk about your involvement with our girls."

"And we won't be having any conversation about that. I know my rights and I'm no idiot. I needn't stay for this pathetic inquisition. Officer, unlock the doors." Moreno didn't move, Cory laughed.

"Officer Moreno, I'll have your badge if you don't obey me. I am ready to leave."

"At this point, sir, if you choose to leave, it will be with me in handcuffs." Oldfather was completely nonplussed.

"What the fuck are you talking about."

"Attempted murder."

"Is this a joke? Yes, I got a call from the girl. She told me to meet her behind the property to go hunting, something I liked to do, but she didn't show up. Her sister Mary, that girl killed herself. As for Dory's real killer, the ballistics confirmed—"

Moreno finished his sentence for him. "Confirmed it wasn't your gun. I know, I have the murder weapon now, and it isn't yours; that's true. However I will be taking you and Woody in for other charges."

The supervisor snorted and snapped at Moreno. "You have lost your mind."

Pari had been watching Madrone, and he was steaming. Each new revelation seemed to have made things worse. His face was flushed, and it was visible mostly in his huge nose and the pulsing vein on his thick neck.

He muttered to himself and then finally shouted at Oldfather. "El diablo, that is what you are. Tu! You have led me down this path of lies and dreams, and now I am a party to your filth." He spat at the supervisor—hugely and accurately. George Oldfather recoiled as if he had been shot and hastily wiped the sputum from his face.

Cory sighed. "Enough of this pantomime...It is time for the rest of our guests to come forward. Spike, Pari, please unmask and join us."

As Pari removed his mask, he saw several things happen almost simultaneously. Woody stood and shouted, "Hijo de puta!" The supervisor grabbed Dolores, pulled her up out of her chair, and held her, his left arm cinched around her neck, his right hand holding a gun to her head. Rupert and Dana both pushed their chairs back and ducked under the table and Rupert shouted, "What the fuck!" Evy stood up, as if to guard the exit towards the kitchen. Spike stepped back from Oldfather, and Woody began fiddling with something in his pocket.

Officer Moreno had also stood, pulling his gun. "George, what are you doing? You can't get out of here. This only makes things worse."

Oldfather glanced at Woody. "Press that fucking button, you idiot."

Moreno spoke again, "I recovered your gun this morning. I also have a witness who saw you toss it out the window of your Humvee coming down Redington Pass. Your fingerprints are all over it, and I've traced your tracks back to the cave-in, where I found additional evidence. Both you and Woody will be held for the attempted murder of Pari Workingboxwalla and Spike Smith."

On hearing this Woody pulled the remote from his pocket and a part of the floor behind the men opened up to reveal a staircase going down to the wine cellar. Pari knew that the tunnels below the house went under the dining room but this was a surprise to most of the rest of the group. Cory seemed unmoved and unsurprised by everything. In stead, while all this was going on he swirled his wine and took a sip, dabbing his lips with his napkin afterward.

Oldfather tightened his hold on Dolores. "We are also prepared," he growled. "I suggest you put your gun down, Philip, unless you would like to see a little blood at the dinner table."

Cory finally spoke, "Please, no blood. Why don't you abandon the histrionics, George? Besides, life as you knew it is over. I am sure by the morning your accounts will be frozen."

"My accounts?"

"Yes, even the shell corporations. You will not be charged only with attempted murder. You see, I know all about the purchases you made and the land sales later on. It's called fraud. Have a seat,

I've prepared a rack of lamb over forbidden rice.   Seemed appropriate. You ought to have a good meal before you go to jail."

Just then, Dolores brought her fist down hard just below George Oldfather's gut, crushing his testicles. His gun went off but it was no longer pointed at Dolores's head, instead, the bullet penetrated Woody Madrone, and that mountain of a man went down. His hand covered the wound in his gut ineffectively, as the blood continued to flow. Dolores broke free and Spike pushed himself in front of her. The supervisor took off down the steps while Pari picked up the remote Woody had used to open the wine cellar. He pressed it, sealing George Oldfather in the cellar below. Pari had recalled that after Woody's earlier break in, Cory had installed security gates in the tunnels, which all locked when the command was given to shut an exit like this one. *It sure feels good to know that snake can't get away,* he thought.

Rupert and Dana were already working on Woody, but Pari could see it was probably too late. Carole Anne had taken his head into her lap and was stroking his hair. He looked at her and said, "She called me Papa, it is true?" Carole Anne nodded and began softly singing to him in Spanish, "Pero todo sea por ti. Ya se que cada cual tiene su precio pero el mio esta en tu pecho, desde el dia en que te vi, Y se que tienes confiscada mi alma." Pari knew the tune from a movie he had seen last year with Dory, Hasta Los Huesos. The song in it, "La Llorona" was all about accepting death. It seemed such a strange thing to hear that song sung by Dory's mother to her father.

Cory stood and softly cursed, "Cabron."

Chapter 32: Stop the Madness

After the police and the ambulance left, Cory, Dolores, Carole Anne, Spike, Philip Moreno and Pari gathered in the library. Evy accompanied Woody in the ambulance but had called in on the way to tell them he'd died in transit. The rest of the paid staff had left. Pari's clients went home once they knew the sale would go forward. Cory reminded them that even though Woody had died, his estate was still bound to go through with the sale. The transfer of the deed would be good, even after his death. Also, he was Woody's executor, and there were no other heirs besides Carole Anne. She looked shocked.

"I can't believe that Woody kept me in his will, as his heir, after all these years."

Pari thought she might cry, but she tougher it out.

Cory touched her shoulder as he spoke. "Cass, I have to ask you if you have any objections, as his heir, or if we may proceed."

"I am in agreement with the sale."

Carole Anne had little to say after hearing that and appeared deeply absorbed to Pari. He asked Cory about the outstanding Estate for Life but Dolores answered.

"Young man, you must have it. Didn't you know? Dory called me the day she died to make sure I had mailed a letter to you. She'd given it to me a few days before. You must have received it. She wanted to be sure everything was taken care of. That is why she called your client, to let him know there wouldn't be a problem. That is what I was arguing with her about, I was trying to persuade her not to confront Oldfather. She was going to expose him. I wanted her to keep silent and keep the deed. But she insisted on giving it to Pari."

"What do you mean? I don't have the deed."

Cory spoke up, "What about the letter you received?" Pari had all but forgotten the envelope Dory had asked him to open on his birthday, but it took him only a few moments to locate it. He opened it and was astonished to see that she had passed the Estate for Life on to him. He asked Carole Anne if she would like it back but she just shook her head no. So Cory helped Pari draw up a quit claim to his clients, giving up his estate for life to them and Dolores notarized the transfer.

Dolores went on, "Dory didn't want to make problems for anyone, really. I drove out to Scorpion Path that day because I thought she sounded suicidal."

Spike chimed in, "I thought so too, but when I got there we fought. She had a gun and I took it."

Carole Anne looked up, "The gun I took from you?"

"Yes, she said she'd borrowed it from you to go hunting. I took it away from her because I was afraid of what kind of hunting she might do."

"And then I took it from you...I couldn't understand why you had my gun, I thought you'd stolen it. I thought you might have meant some harm." She looked aside.

Cory looked at Philip and nodded. "Yes, now is the time," he said.

Officer Moreno produced the weapon.

"Is this your gun?" he asked Carole Anne.

"Yes, but how..."

Cory interrupted. "It is a sad tale told too often, never remembered and always shocking. Unfailingly we hurt the ones we love, in our very attempt to protect them and ourselves." He walked to the sideboard and poured a snifter of Armagnac, offering everyone a glass. Dolores and Spike joined in the libation, but the rest declined. *This was Cory's way,* Pari thought, *not so much to know everything, but to point to the source of the knowledge. He put people together who had the answers required.*

Cory spoke again. "George Oldfather blackmailed or fooled some of you to get his way. He threatened Dolores with the arrest of her girls for drugs." He turned to her, "Isn't that why you were willing to notarize all those sales with straw buyers?"

She answered quietly, "Yes."

"Then he blackmailed the girls, threatening your exposure to get what he wanted from them. He played variations on this theme with you, Spike, to keep Dory in line." Spike nodded, "Woody, for all his faults, fell into Oldfather's web innocently enough, but once he was in he couldn't get out. That was why he wanted to sell his house: to get out of the trouble he found himself in."

Carole Anne looked confused, "Cory, I don't understand. If George Oldfather didn't kill Dory..."

The realization struck her and she let out a wail so pitiful it broke Pari's heart. Dolores went to her and held her. Dolores's own eyes were flowing, and her sobs were guttural and ragged, Pari could see she had been aware of the facts for a while. There they were, two Medea's, two women who had inadvertently killed their own children. They held each other in their sorrow.

"Cass, she was headed for death without you. Her plan was to confront the man she felt had ruined her life. That stray bullet from your gun was the instrument, but another would have taken its place. I do not believe that George Oldfather would have put up with her threats." Dolores spoke up then.

"Dory and I argued minutes before she died; the last words I had with her were awful. I told her to leave Oldfather to me. She told me I was incapable of dealing with him and I said she could not come back till she stopped using, The last words she said to me, 'Don't worry because I'm never coming back,' made me furious. Then I saw you, Carole, through the atrium glass. I was so angry you were there—I decided to confront you. When the alarm sounded, I thought I had set it off. Then, later, when your gun went off and you dropped it, I took it. I was not sure if you had killed her, or Oldfather. So I took the gun to threaten him. He ran and I followed, but he lost me at the picnic area, where he'd parked his vehicle. Later I followed him to the All Souls procession. I thought there I could confront him and you, but I nearly killed you, and then I lost the gun. I am so sorry."

Spike was quietly weeping and Pari went to him and asked if he was okay.

"No," he said, "If I had not brought her to Oldfather, and to the drugs she would not have died."

Cory stirred, "But you didn't kill her. We all had a hand in her death."

"I know I played a part." Said Pari, "She called me that morning and asked me to take the day off with her so she could talk some things through. If I had done that, Dory would be here today, but I turned her down and told her I was too busy."

Cory sighed. "Guns. Almost everyone had one, but the only people shot were killed in error. Everyone could have played a role to stop the madness, but none of us did. We can choose to grieve and wallow in self pity, or we can take these events as a lesson—to listen to our dear ones when they have something to say, to really hear them and love them while they are with us. If we can take that to heart, then the death of these two has meaning and worth. Otherwise, they both died in vain, another story of random chaos." All were silent for a moment and then he continued, "Officer, I do not know if you feel the need to pursue this matter, but in my opinion the guilty have been found and justice has been meted out for all of us that played a part. If you are willing, I will take that gun and dispose of it, and it will never have use again."

Philip Moreno nodded and then took Dolores and Carole Anne home. Spike and Pari stayed up late into the night talking through the events of the last few weeks, and then Spike too went home. Pari had a difficult night's sleep and dreamed of Dory. They were traveling in her jeep and he woke in the morning hearing her laughter. The dream seemed so real that, illogical as it was, he thought she might still be alive and just hiding.

Chapter 33 A Feeling of Dread: Afterword

Pari's dreams of Dory continued. Sometimes they seemed real, so vivid, he couldn't shake the feelings they left him with—often for the remainder of the day. He tried to set them aside by working hard, but he had limited success. He'd had a successful closing with the Brooks the following week and it seemed to him everyone was happy but himself. After the closing he felt lost and worthless, a letdown he didn't expect. He hoped it was just a matter of time until these feelings began to fade. *But how long will it take?*

Cory had created a "New Agent" training class and asked him to review it. He applied himself to that, recognizing many of his mistakes in his first sale, but his heart wasn't in it. He'd called his mother and father, but they'd seen the reports about his incarceration, and the newspaper brought out the most lurid details —so thus far they were cool to him. Dana and Rupert invited him out and overtly expressed their joy in owning the place, but he found it depressing and felt like a stranger at their table. They were oblivious —they told him they were planning to have a grand house warming sometime around Christmas or New Years. He'd later received the invitation, but could not bring himself to respond. *Perhaps tomorrow*, he thought. *Of course I must go. I should want to go, but I can't imagine being in that house again.* He couldn't picture himself having a party on the very spot where Dory had died.

One night he'd had a particularly elaborate and disturbing dream that he was living in the mountains in a cabin in the Catalina's. He was on the porch admiring the thrum of hummingbirds zooming by his ears as they robbed nectar from a feeder hanging from the porch railing...a bright red bottle, swinging —dripping sticky blood red syrup. *I must fix that!* He'd thought.

He stood up and walked into the forest. Around him massive pines, each three or four feet in diameter, towered to the skies. The sun, filtering in patches through the canopy, was hot on his skin, though the breeze was cool. The only sounds he could hear were the soft crush of old pine needles under his feet, the far whisper of the breeze in the pine tops and an occasional bird song. Columbines and Irises clustered around the massive trunks, and the scent of those flowers mixed with pine.

His dog came running toward him, though he had no dog in real life. In this dream Pari had always owned the dog. "Founder!" he called, and knelt to receive him. Founder licked his face and nuzzled him. The dog was white and brindled with grey spots that shown through his translucent short fur. He was a handsome beast, tall, almost 90 pounds of muscle, bright brown eyes and a sweet disposition—but now he barked at Pari with some urgency. Pari asked him what was wrong and he gave a yip and bounded into the woods. Pari followed fast and Founder led him to a person sitting on the ground. Pari could not tell who it was.

She, or he, sat faced away from Pari. Her back, or his, was covered with mud. A stream flowed beside them and Pari pulled him, or her, up and washed the mud from her body—or his. Who is she, who is he? The confusion didn't matter. When he was clean, she kissed him. A sweet and innocent kiss. After the kiss, Pari looked into his eyes and was overcome with desire. Filled with strength, he grabbed him, or her. Pari was potent and strong and had an urgent need to express his burning passion. He took her head in both his hands and pulled his mouth to his with force. He was famished and hungry for the taste of her, of him? In his urgency he, no she must have bitten his lip because the taste of blood, salty, coppery and bright, flooded his mouth. Yet this only increased Pari's desire. He kissed him or her again, yes, and yes, he kissed him or her deeper and more forcefully.

When he came up for air, with a shock he saw he was kissing Dory. She looked at him with frightened, pleading eyes. She held two Tarot cards in front of her, and she gave them to him. He looked at them and saw a card of a young man with a bindle-staff on a cliff, and another of the grim reaper. He woke then, in a sweat, and could not shake a feeling of dread—nor the feeling that the dream was real.

Spike's phone call came shortly after he woke. He said he wanted to take Pari to see a medium. Pari was not a big believer in ghosts and said no, but Spike told him three things that changed his mind. First, the medium lived in a cabin on Mount Lemmon, in the virgin woods of Bear Hollow. She was an old Wiccan named Saraphina, with a penchant for the Tarot. She made philters from ancient recipes. Spike knew her from a Qigong class and she'd invited him and Pari up to see her on the mountain. Spike wanted to go that day, before the first snow, before the hummingbirds left. Second, he'd mentioned to her that Pari was a real estate agent. She'd said that Pari should come along because she might want to list her house with him. Third, Spike wanted to bring his new dog—a dog who had found him yesterday, a big, white, spotted, short haired Old Danish Pointer who he had decided to call "Founder."

Spike's words sent a chill through Pari's body, and a feeling of dread washed over him. Nevertheless, Pari knew he had to go.

To be continued in "Rites of Survivorship."

22001248R00151